Kaleigh

A Story of Patience

Lisa Washington

Library of Congress Control Number:

ISBN-13: 978-1-953205-00-1
ISBN-10: 1-953205-00-1

Washington Way Publishing
P.O. Box 7231
Fishers, IN 46038
Printed in the United States of America
www.thewashingtonwayllc.com

DEDICATION

For All Sisters ~ Biological and Un-Biological

Caleigh & Leighanna

Tierra & Tamera

LaVeta, Sheleta & Lauren

Brenda & April

Patricia, Brenda, Mary, Linda, & Laura

Ashley & TriNiece

Carleigh, Jai & Jaice

The Shobe Sisters

The McCray Sisters

The Teasley Sisters

Be joyful in hope, patient in affliction, faithful in prayer.
Romans 12:12 NIV

ACKNOWLEDGMENTS

God Almighty

My wonderful husband Mr. Coach Washington

My Sisters ~ Leslie, Penelopia, Ta'Neia, Filipa, Yolanda, Taura, Lena,

Rasheda Randle of Ivy League Consulting

Shannan Harper

Chapter 1

Poe entered her office, balancing her cell phone between her ear and shoulder while carrying three bags of Thai food. She was partially listening to the person on the phone and trying to get some assistance with the food before she dropped the bags. Occasionally, she would throw in an "okay" or "alright" to let the person on the phone know she was still listening, but she wasn't paying attention to the caller.

Janice, the office receptionist, was also on the phone and couldn't leave her desk to help. Instead, Janice balled up a piece of paper and threw it across the office at one of the real estate agents sitting at his desk, not doing anything.

"I'm sorry, Ms. Hammond," Carl said, jumping up to grab the food. "I didn't see you walk in."

Poe nodded, handing him the bags of food, and followed him to the back of the office, where the kitchen was located.

To the person on the phone, she said, "Okay sister, I'm back in the office. I have to go now."

"Fine. I know you weren't listening to me anyway," Karleigh cried.

"I was listening to you." Poe gave Carl the hand signal for talking too much while pointing to the phone. "We are going to meet at the bridal boutique on Saturday."

"And what else?" Karleigh asked.

"You got me. That was all I heard. But, I promise to be all ears on Saturday. Love you, sister." Poe quickly ended the call before her sister could start talking again.

Ever since her older sister, Karleigh, got engaged to the super attractive owner of Sharper Image Barbershops, Poe had been driving everyone crazy with wedding stuff. She understood that wedding planning could cause some women to go insane, but she had never thought it would be Karleigh.

Of the four Hammond sisters, Karleigh was the one who usually cried when faced with adversity, but would also quickly bounce back, picking herself up and powering forward. Now, she was frustrating everyone with wedding details that no one cared about. Being the sister closest in age to Karleigh, Poe endured every lengthy, detailed conversation.

Poe had decided to treat everyone in her office to lunch. The K. Hammond Real Estate office was celebrating snagging a high-end client. Thai cuisine was her favorite, so she ordered Pad Pak, several spring rolls, and drunken noodles for everyone to share. She made herself a plate with healthy portions and then retreated to the sanctuary of her private office.

Kaleigh Patience Hammond started calling herself Poe around the time her baby sister, Kyna, was born. She hated having a K name. Her parents were Kyra and Kevin, and her other sister was Karmyn. Her grandmother would always get them confused and just started calling them Girl One, Two, Three, and Four, based upon their birth order.

Most people also confused Poe with her sister Karleigh. They were the same height, had the same caramel complexion, and until recently, they had the same long, jet black hair. Poe, needing a change, cut her hair into a shoulder-length bob. It also didn't help that their names were only one letter off, and they were only 18 months apart in age, looking more like twins.

Poe started her career in real estate because she loved everything about houses. She would sit for hours drawing floor plans of her future homes. When she wasn't watching HGTV, she would read books of all kinds. Once, a librarian gave her a book by Edgar Allen Poe, introducing her to detective fiction. She enjoyed reading about C. Auguste Dupin so much that she named herself after the author who introduced her to another world.   Growing up, she insisted that everyone call her Poe and refused to answer anyone who didn't address her as such. Eventually, the name stuck. Only her Grandmother would still call her Kaleigh.

She took her first bite of the drunken noodles and then turned her computer on. She had to prepare for her meeting with Mr. Morgan Hawkins. He was a hotelier and looking to build his next hotel in the city. He didn't build fancy, large hotels; he was known for quaint, historic boutique types. His vision was to convert an existing building and restore its historic charm.

Poe loved that idea and jumped at the opportunity to work with him. She spent many evenings, after regular working hours, working on her proposal. It took the Hawkins group six-months to respond. In the time it took them to review her proposal, she anxiously awaited a decision. She still remembered getting that award letter. No one was in the office to hear her scream and shout. Thankful for the biggest opportunity of her career, she couldn't stop praising God. The holy ghost moved through her right in her office.

Still stuffing noodles in her mouth, she checked her emails, deleting the spam and advertisements that filled her inbox. One email caught her eye, but she decided not to open it yet. She had too much to do to prepare for Mr. Hawkins' arrival.

"Poe, are you available?" Janice asked after knocking on her door.

"Yes, Jan, come on in," she responded.

Janice had been her receptionist and business mentor since she opened her office. They met while working for another real estate broker when Poe was just starting out in the industry. Janice had owned a few other businesses before trying her hands at real estate. When Poe decided she wanted to go out on her own, Janice was right beside her, giving her advice and keeping her motivated.

They celebrated together when Poe sold her first house as K. Hammond Real Estate. Now that Janice had retired, she worked part-time as the receptionist and office assistant. Poe would be lost without Jan's friendship and business expertise.

Closing the door behind her, Jan eased into one of the chairs in front of Poe's desk.

"Now you know I am not one to gossip, but the rumor around here is that you are going to let Carl work on the Hawkins account. Tell me that isn't so?"

Poe smiled, "Carl is capable. He can help with a big client."

"The boy hasn't sold a house in over three months. He comes in here, sits on that computer, and talks on his phone. He hasn't even shown a house in the past two weeks."

Carl Atwater started off as an eager go-getter. In the past few months, he had been slacking and not working to his potential. Poe had noticed it, but since her agents worked on commission, she didn't worry about it too much. She thought he was in a slump and would bounce back.

"I hear what you're saying, Jan, but maybe this is what he needs to get out of this rut he seems to be in." She noticed Jan looked at her with a frown of disbelief. "If it makes you feel better, I'll monitor him closely for the first couple of weeks."

"That does make me feel better." Janice stood and used her hands to smooth her skirt down. "By the way, the conference room is ready for your meeting with Mr. Hawkins."

"Thank you, Jan. I would be lost without you."

"I know you would," Janice smiled and returned her desk.

Poe continued to eat her lunch while preparing for her meeting. Everything had to be perfect for the Hawkins Group. Her agency needed this client, and she needed this win. She finished her meal before asking Carl into her office. Together, they worked on the information they had gathered about a few buildings in the area that may be of interest to Mr. Hawkins.

Despite Jan's concerns, the two of them worked well together. Carl was usually enthusiastic about his job but noticed that recently, he had been slacking off more and more. Poe met Carl after he passed the real estate licensing exam. He was exuberant and eager to learn the ropes. Nowadays, he was careless and forgetful. There was something else going on with Carl that was causing him to become lax with his work. Poe would have to ask him about it later, especially if he continued the way he was going.

A few hours later, Mr. Hawkins arrived at the office. Jan escorted him and his team into the conference room, then went to notify Poe.

She knocked on the door before entering. "Poe, Mr. Hawkins is here. That man is fine. If I were a few years younger," she said, fanning herself.

"Janice, let's be professional," Poe laughed while gathering the last of her documents.

"I was professional. But, let me tell you this, his staff is fine too. It's like, he only brought the best of the best with him."

"Are they all men?"

"One lady. She ain't bad looking, either. Keep Carl on his leash," Janice tossed over her shoulder as she left the room.

Poe had known Carl to be distracted by a pretty face. If she didn't know any better, she might believe that Carl was having trouble with women. Maybe that was why he hasn't been on his game in the past few weeks.

Poe was heading in the direction of the conference room when she was stopped by Angela, one of her new agents.

"Poe, if you need anything at all. You let me know," Angela said, adjusting her dress to show a little more cleavage than what was appropriate for the office.

"I guess news of Mr. Hawkins being attractive has made it around the office," Poe responded.

"Attractive doesn't even begin to put butter on the bread. You just remember I'm right here. Eager and ready to yearn…I mean, learn."

Poe thought, *I just bet you are ready.* She was stopped twice more by other agents before actually making it into the conference room.

"I'm sorry to keep you waiting, Mr. Hawkins, I had a small fire to put out," Poe spoke after placing all of her folders on the table. She then looked up and saw three gorgeous men and one beautiful woman. Janice wasn't exaggerating at all. This group could easily pass for fashion models.

Mr. Morgan Hawkins stood and extended his hand to Poe. The other two men stood alongside him.

"Ms. Hammond. I'm Mr. Morgan Hawkins. This is my brother and business partner, John Hawkins. My sister, Melissa Hawkins, and this is my older brother, Dr. Grant Hawkins."

The siblings all favored one another. The brothers all stood at least six feet, three inches, and Melissa was right there with them at about five foot, ten inches. They all shared the same skin tone and bone structure, but Grant and Melissa had eyes the color of golden topaz, while John and Morgan had deep chocolate-colored brown eyes.

"It is a pleasure to meet each of you," Poe greeted each of them. When she went to reach for Dr. Hawkins' hand, she was stopped by the intensity in which he was looking at her. She felt like the only other person in the room. When he released her hand, the connection was also broken. She was grateful for that, or she may have been the one who wasn't acting professionally.

Poe exhaled at the moment Carl entered the room carrying bottled waters for everyone. "Please be seated. Have you met my assistant, Carl?"

"Yes, we have. Thank you," Morgan said to Carl, taking the water from his hand.

"Great, let's get this meeting started. We have found some great buildings for you to take a look at." Poe handed each of them a portfolio. For the next couple of hours, the six of them went over building after building. Poe was taking notes and answering questions. The entire time, she could feel Grant's eyes on her. With every step around the room, he was watching her.

*****

This woman is beautiful, Grant thought. He watched her command the room and talk about buildings with ease. When she entered the room, the hairs on the back of his neck immediately stood at attention. Her beauty took his breath away, and when he held her hand in a handshake, he felt a tingle up his arm. He also felt her slight shiver, and instinctively knew she felt the charge, too.

Grant was enthralled in her wealth of knowledge about the buildings she presented. She knew the history, ownership, and usage of each location. Some of the information went back over 100 years. He was amazed at her detail; she had broken down utility costs and potential insurance premiums. Her research on each building was meticulous.

"I have a question?"

"Sure. What's your question, Dr. Hawkins?"

"Building A is near the hospital. That area is being re-developed for more residential, but Building E is located near the Amphitheater. Lots of shopping and restaurants going up in that area. Wouldn't those be the top options?"

"Dr. Hawkins, I can see how you would think that. But, let's look at the taxes in each area. The hospital area has been re-zoned for mixed-use, and having a hotel near a hospital would be an asset to patients and families; however, the increase in taxes for the area would be double those in the Hawthorne Park area."

"The Hawthorne Park area only has the historic district going for it."

"That may be so, Dr. Hawkins, but I believe it is the historic environment that the Hawkins Group is looking for, am I wrong?" She turned to Morgan with her question.

"Ms. Hammond, you are correct," Morgan agreed with her.

"Please, call me Kaleigh."

Grant wanted to call her later for dinner and maybe more. He admired she wasn't able to be rattled and really knew her market. John and Melissa both agreed with Kaleigh and thought the building near the hospital was worth a look regardless of the increase in taxes.

They had been in the meeting for so long, Morgan suggested taking everyone out for dinner. That was a great idea. Grant needed more time in her presence, preferably alone, but he would take a restaurant to start.

"Why don't we head over to Lorenzo's? I hear the food is absolutely delicious," Grant offered.

"I'm sorry, Mr. Hawkins, but I will have to pass. I would like to start the paperwork for these two buildings. I think we can make a lower offer on Building C. With some negotiation, I'm confident that might be your best win."

"Ms. Hammond, I'm sorry you won't be joining us, but please keep my team informed. John will be your point of contact. Melissa and I will be returning to New York."

"It was a pleasure to meet each of you." Kaleigh escorted the group out of the conference room.

Grant wanted to stay back and talk to Kaleigh. But, his brother kept nudging him forward and eventually out of the building.

"Geesh, Grant, can you be any more obvious?" Melissa laughed.

"What?" Grant threw his hands up in the air. "What can I say? She is absolutely beautiful."

"You've seen beautiful women before. You've even dated a few. Why is she different?" John asked.

"This one has a job and brains, that's what makes her different," Morgan laughed and got into the SUV that waited for them in front of the building.

John and Melissa waited a full second before laughing at Grant and following their brother into the SUV. Grant had to admit that his siblings knew him well. He was attracted to a pretty face and a killer body…brains not essential.

"I'll meet you guys at the restaurant," Grant told them and started walking toward his car. He had been working in this city since his residency, loving the small-town charm and friendly people. Morgan had become interested in developing a hotel when Grant couldn't stop talking about the area and its potential.

Dr. Grant Hawkins was a leading obstetrics and gynecology physician, specializing in fertility. Before medical school, Grant had been a skinny nerd who couldn't buy a date. He focused all of his energy into his studies and graduated from high school and college at the top of his class.

He was accepted into several medical schools, but settled on Meharry in Tennessee, always wanting to attend a Historical Black College or University. There he grew into a man, a handsome man, according to the ladies. He didn't know if it was his potential as a doctor or his physical attributes. In high school, he was 6'2" and 150lbs. In medical school, he began working out in the gym and gained 40 lbs. of muscle.

Women would flock to him. First, it was one of the other med students; then, he attracted a few of the staff members at the school. While those ladies never approached him, he could hear their whispered conversations.

One thing was for sure, he was unusually attracted to Kaleigh Hammond, and he was determined to find out why.

Chapter 2

After a long week of working on accounting issues at the agency, Poe was ready for a weekend of relaxation with her sisters. She would be meeting them at the spa Saturday morning before they all headed over to the bridal store to select their bridesmaids' gowns for Karleigh's wedding. Poe promised Karleigh she would show up in the morning with a smile on her face.

Since her meeting with the Grant's, Poe had been buried in contracts, tax papers, building liens, and inspector reports. She was waiting for one last inspection report before submitting an offer on the building in Hawthorne Park.

Karleigh had tried to call Poe every evening to talk about the wedding planning, and Poe had to blow her off each time. She loved her sister and wanted to be all-in for the wedding details, but this was an important time at the K. Hammond Real Estate Agency. Once she was able to get the offer submitted, Poe would be glad to hand the rest over to Carl.

Bright and early Saturday morning, the Hammond sisters arrived for their quarterly spa treatments. They always started

Sister Spa Day with thirty minutes in the sauna to relax and release. The sauna was also the time that included their sister talks when they talked about what was going on in each of their lives, the good and the bad. They listened, then offered each other support and advice.

"Who wants to start?" Karleigh asked.

"I'll start," Kyna jumped in. "Ever since I got assigned to pretty boy, Dr. Wonderful's team, I've had to fight off every female nurse in the building. And some male nurses too. Sure, he is attractive, if you like that smug, arrogant type. Ugh, these women act like they have never seen a good-looking man before."

"Kyna, it can't be that bad," Karmyn responded.

"Oh, really? Last week, one of the operating room nurses asked to take me to lunch. I have never met this woman before. I tried to decline, but she insisted. We met in the cafeteria, where she brought three of her girlfriends to question me about Dr. Ego."

The three sisters laughed. Poe thought, if Dr. Ego looked anything like Dr. Hawkins, she could understand why the nurses were acting a little foolish. When he shook her hand at the meeting, she felt a quick jolt up her arm. If she got that feeling from a handshake, what would she feel if he kissed her?

Karleigh broke into Poe's thoughts and asked Kyna, "Do you want off of his service?"

"Heck no. He has a brilliant mind and has focused much of his career on improving fertility options for women. I am actually grateful that I was selected to be on his team. I just wish the job description included personal security. Oh, and check this out, us nurses also have to field his phone calls. So many women calling, leaving all types of racy messages."

The sisters looked one to the other and then burst out laughing again at Kyna. Being the baby of the family, she was spoiled and coddled beyond belief. Sometimes the older sisters wondered if she was still a virgin. Especially when she made comments and funny faces about sex.

"Well, I had a great, but chaotic week," Poe said. "I met with a client who will be investing hugely into our city. His multi-million-dollar deal will definitely have me seeing high six figures."

"Congratulations, Sister, I'm so proud of you," Karmyn told her.

"Is that why you weren't paying any attention to me on the phone the other day? And, why you kept sending my calls to voicemail?" Karleigh asked.

"I was paying attention. Sort of."

Again, the sisters laughed at each other and continued to talk about their lives. Spa day was the only time they could openly talk to one another at the same time. Usually, they would tell one sister something and then have to repeat the conversation to the others. The only other time they were all together was at Sunday dinners at their parents' house. There was no way the sisters would speak freely around their parents or their grandmother.

After their time in the sauna, they received full-body massages and then continued relaxing in the cooling room with their drinks of choice. Karleigh always got a Tequila Sunrise. Karmyn didn't drink alcohol, so she opted for a strawberry smoothie. Kyna usually stuck with the traditional mimosa, while Poe would often get a glass of Riesling. But, this visit, Poe wanted something a lot stronger. She decided on a margarita with a twist. The twist was an extra shot of tequila.

"Poe, are you sure everything is okay? It's not like you to drink heavily in the middle of the day?" Karmyn asked.

"I'm fine. I just have a lot on my mind. This client can make or break me," she sighed. "I know I submitted a great proposal, that's why he selected my company, but If I fail…"

"Sister! You are not going to fail. Don't talk like that," Karmyn said.

Poe had been putting on a strong front for her staff and her sisters. But, deep down inside, she was allowing fear to seep into her mind. Too many what-ifs were causing her to second guess her gift. Poe was constantly telling herself she was experienced, and she could make this deal work.

"You're right. Words have life. I will not speak that into existence." Poe took a deep breath and slowly exhaled. "I don't know why I'm tripping. I got this."

Sipping on another mimosa, Kyna chimed in, "You sure do. Hammond sisters don't do anything halfway."

The sisters continued their traditional spa treatments with facials, manicures, and pedicures. Afterward, they had lunch at one of their favorite restaurants. This month, it was Kyna's turn to pick the restaurant. Poe was happy to have extra cash on hand because Kyna always chose the most swanky and expensive restaurants in the city.

"Sisters, you will love this place. I just found out about this little gem," Kyna started talking about the restaurant. Poe was only half listening because she had just received a text message from her office. The initial documents on the building were ready to be reviewed. She quickly sent a text to Carl, instructing him to review the documents and prepare them for Mr. Hawkins.

"Poe, are you working on our Saturday?" Karmyn asked.

"Just a quick text. This project is huge for me, and I cannot ignore this." Dropping her phone into her purse and clapping her hands together, Poe said, "See, no more. Now, how expensive is this restaurant?"

"It's very reasonable." Kyna rolled her eyes, and Poe returned the action.

The sisters arrived at a new restaurant located not too far from the hospital where Kyna worked. The décor was reminiscent of a French bistro. The pictures of the Eiffel Tower and the Arc de Triomphe were indications of the Parisian style. They were immediately seated in the middle of the restaurant with views in every direction. Poe was sitting across from Kyna, who had a direct line of vision to the front door. Karmyn sat next to Kyna and across from Karleigh.

Wedding plans were being discussed in great detail when Kyna turned up her nose.

"What's wrong with you?" Poe asked her.

"It's him. Dr. Ego."

Karleigh and Poe swiftly turned around, scraping their chairs against the tiled floor, not caring that they were obviously looking at the man who just entered. Poe's heart sank when she realized that Kyna's Dr. Ego was none other than Dr. Grant Hawkins. She had hoped to not see him again so soon.

They made direct eye contact, and Poe quickly turned away. "Dr. Hawkins, is your Dr. Ego?" Poe asked Kyna.

"You know him?"

"I met him and his family a few days ago. His brother is Morgan Hawkins of the Hawkins Group. The big contract I just won," she whispered.

Karleigh and Karmyn had no shame, openly staring at Grant. They then returned their attention to the table, looking back and forth from Poe to Kyna as they talked.

"Why do you seem less than enthused to see him?" Kyna asked Poe.

"You're full of questions, aren't you?" Poe responded, closing her eyes and taking a deep breath.

"Don't get your panties twisted in a knot." The two bickered.

Karmyn interrupted, "Don't look now; the Doctor is headed this way."

Poe suddenly felt anxious and tried to calm her nerves by pasting on a fake smile, but her attempt at being genuine was somewhere near 10%. During their previous meeting, she could feel his vibes being directed at her. It was a feeling she couldn't quite describe. He wouldn't stop staring at her, and it unnerved her during the presentation. When he invited her to dinner, she had quickly turned him down. Poe didn't trust herself to remain professional around him. Dr. Hawkins was a temptation she didn't need in her life.

"Hello, ladies," Grant said as he arrived at the table. His smooth, deep voice reverberated through Poe, and she couldn't turn around to face him.

Karmyn and Karleigh returned his greeting and openly gawked at him. Kyna said hi but ignored him by pulling out her cell phone. Poe wasn't shocked that Karmyn or Karleigh would respond in that manner. They both appreciated a well-dressed, good-looking man.

"Ms. Hammond. How are you today?" he directed his question to Poe.

"Just fine, Dr. Hawkins. And how are you?" she responded without turning around. Poe kept her eyes looking downward at the napkin she was stretching in her lap.

"I'm better now that I have seen you today." Grant leaned closer to Poe and whispered, but loud enough for her sisters to hear, "Do you think we can talk about business for a minute... privately?"

Poe realized her sisters weren't saying anything, and when she looked around the table, they all sat open-jawed, staring at her.

What was their problem? She thought.

She turned in her seat to look at Grant and quickly realized that it was a mistake. He had those eyes that called to you and had you thinking crazy thoughts of forever.

"This is my time with my sisters. We lead pretty busy lives, and I think it would be very inappropriate for me to discuss business with you without your brother present. Give my office a call on Monday. I'm sure Carl Atwater will be able to answer any questions you have." She turned in her seat, effectively dismissing him.

Instead of appearing offended, he simply straightened up to his full height, smiled, and said, "I will do just that. Ladies, have a wonderful lunch."

Once Grant was away from the table, Karleigh asked Poe, "What's stuck up your butt? That fine man wanted to speak with you privately; you should have jumped at the opportunity." Taking a sip from her water glass, she stared at her sister.

The last thing Poe wanted or needed in her life was a man to complicate things. Her business was vital to her and her sense of solitude. Poe enjoyed living alone and having space. She couldn't imagine having to share her time and space with anyone else at this time in her life. Instead of answering her sister, she reached for the menu and held it up, blocking the stares from Kyna and Karmyn.

"We will table this discussion until later," Kyna added.

*****

Grant was delighting in his luck to find the beautiful real estate agent in the very restaurant he loved to frequent, sitting with one of his best nurses. Finding out they were sisters could be good or bad. He knew the reputation he had seemed to have followed him from hospital to hospital, but most of it was unfounded rumors.

He was often photographed and seen with beautiful Hollywood type women, but none of them stirred him enough to want more after the first date. One woman came close. She made it to a fourth date before he ended their connection. She was a lawyer he had met while serving on the board of a non-profit organization a few years ago. Her intellect drew him in, but insecurities drove him away. Due to both of them having busy schedules, they had only gone on four dates in three months. She accused him of cheating before the relationship ever got off the ground.

Since that time, he preferred one-night stands, and the women he was involved with understood that arrangement. Grant didn't have the time to cultivate a relationship; his career and research kept him plenty busy. He remembered something his father once told him. "When you find the right woman, you won't be able to run or use work as an excuse. She will change your heart and have you thinking about life differently." Already, Kaleigh had him thinking of long-term commitments.

The women he usually chose to date were a fleeting thought since meeting Kaleigh. Her knowledge of real estate and self-confidence sucked him all the way in, leaving him wanting to know more about her. Already, his mind was plotting on how to extract personal information from her sister. Nurse Kyna was by far the most competent nurse he had to work with. Other nurses tried to get on his service to flirt with him, but Kyna was the first who wanted to learn.

He was ordering his take-out, but while waiting for his food, he couldn't keep his eyes from their table. Grant could only see the back of Kaleigh's head. He was fascinated with how beautiful her hair was and how he wanted to run his fingers through her curls. Suddenly, he detected a slight motion from one of the sisters at the table. Was she signaling for him to meet her in the back? Grant made direct eye-contact with her, and she again moved her eyes to the side, then she stood and walked in the direction she was hinting.

No one had ever called him clueless, so he followed and met Karmyn near the restrooms.

"What do I owe this honor?"

"My sister is not to be toyed with. Your reputation precedes you, Doctor. I just wanted to give you a warning. One, Kyna, will not give you any information, so don't try. And two, I know people, if you get my drift. Get out of line once with my sister, and you will be sorry."

Karmyn turned away and walked back toward her sisters. Grant lowered his head and chuckled. Her sisters were interesting, and if he ever got a date with Kaleigh Hammond, he felt it would be an adventure. Unexpectedly, there was a piercing scream, Grant looked up to see Kaleigh on the ground, and Kyna kneeled down beside her.

Grant jumped into action as a doctor. He raced toward the table and kneeled beside Kyna. "What's her heart rate?"

"It's elevated. 106 beats per minute," Kyna said. "Sister, raise her feet," she instructed Karmyn.

"What happened? Did she hit her head?" Grant asked.

"No, she started complaining about getting a headache, then she leaned over into me. When I realized she passed out, I lowered her to the floor."

Kaleigh's eyes started to flutter open.

Kyna started softly talking to her. "Hey, Sister, can you hear me?"

Kaleigh moaned a little but didn't say anything.

"Should we call 911?" Karmyn asked.

"The hospital is nearby; if she doesn't come around in 60 seconds, I will carry her over myself."

Kaleigh then whispered for Kyna. "I'm here, Sister. Do you know where you are?" Kyna asked.

Kaleigh fluttered her eyes and then whispered, "In the restaurant. What happened?"

Grant answered her, "You fainted. Do you think you can sit up for me?"

"Yeah, I think so." She leaned on both Kyna and Grant to help her into a sitting position. She looked around and was embarrassed by the commotion she was causing. "My head is killing me."

"Does this happen often?" Grant asked.

"The headaches, yes. Fainting, no."

"I want you to come over to the hospital and get checked out," Grant told her.

"What do you know? You are a gynecologist."

"I'm still a doctor, and I know enough to be concerned." Turning to Kyna, he said, "Make sure we get her into the emergency room right now."

Karleigh and Karmyn were standing by in total awe of the scene unfolding before them. First, they were scared. It was Karleigh who screamed when Poe first passed out. After seeing their baby sister in action, and the gorgeous doctor come to the rescue, both sisters calmed down and allowed the professionals to handle things.

"Don't worry, I'm taking her over there right now," Kyna answered. "Sister, do you think you can stand up?"

Kaleigh struggled to stand and tried to balance herself by grabbing the table. The sunlight coming in through the window was causing her headache to intensify, and she lost her balance, leaning into Grant.

"Kyna, I don't think she can walk across the street. I will carry her over if you can grab my lunch, please."

Karleigh jumped in, "I'll grab your lunch. You just take her over there. We are right behind you."

Kaleigh didn't protest. She was able to hide her face away from the sun by turning into Grant's chest. Even though the pain she was experiencing, Poe was able to appreciate his muscular build and strong arms that carried her like a feather. He smelled good, too, and his voice was soothing in contrast to the pounding her head was causing.

The emergency room was more active than usual. Patients filled the plastic chairs in the small waiting room. Grant walked past the front desk administrator and immediately found an empty room, placing Kaleigh gently on the bed. Kyna moved into action, again, grabbing the blood pressure cuff and a thermometer. "Dr. Hawkins, her BP is 160 over 100, but her pulse is coming down." She snapped a device in Kaleigh's ear. "Her temperature is normal."

"Thank you, nurse."

The door flung opened, and Dr. Rhodes entered, "What is going on here? Dr. Hawkins, I didn't know you were working in my ER today."

"Sorry, Brad. She went down at the restaurant across the street, and I instinctively brought her over."

"I see. Well, this is my ER, and you are not on duty; or you, Nurse Kyna. Both of you and these other ladies can wait in the lobby. Goodbye."

After waiting for what seemed like hours, but in reality, was only 30 minutes, Kaleigh came out from the emergency room into the lobby, walking on her own.

"Poe, are you alright?" Karleigh rushed to her side. Karmyn went to the other side.

"I'm fine. My pressure came down naturally, and the doctor gave me a shot of Toradol. The pain subsided quickly, although not completely gone. I'm going home to rest." She turned to Kyna, "Can you take me home?"

"I will take you home," Grant announced, stepping forward. "I'll catch a taxi back."

"I appreciate you being there for me, but one of my sisters can take me home," Poe snapped back at him.

"Dr. Hawkins, we really do appreciate everything you did, but we got it from here," Karmyn jumped in before Grant could respond.

"Yes, thank you, Dr. Hawkins. I'll see you in the morning," Kyna added.

He was feeling rejected, and that was new for him. The last time Grant felt rejection of any kind was in high school. Even then, he promised himself never to willingly be put in that position again. If this was how women felt the morning after, he wanted no parts of it.

Later that evening, Grant was enjoying a glass of wine with his brother, John, in his hotel suite.

"John, wouldn't it be better to just rent a condo or something?"

"Why? At the hotel, I get room service 24/7, housekeeping, a pool, and a fitness center. If I get a condo, I will have to cook for myself, hire a maid, and get a gym membership. I think this works better for my lifestyle."

The brothers enjoyed living a life of luxury. Their father had invested well, and their mother kept them grounded, but she also had an affinity for the finer things. They grew up going to private schools and having housekeeping staff. Even growing up affluent, their mother made sure they volunteered in several places throughout the year. Their favorite place to volunteer was the family pantry at their church.

Mount Zion Baptist Church had a pantry where families could come and get clothing items, household goods, and food. Grant enjoyed playing with the kids in the nursery while their parents shopped or received prayer and counseling. Working with the kids and babies is where Grant first developed an interest in becoming a doctor. At first, he wanted to be a pediatrician, but in medical school, he switched to obstetrics. He just had an overwhelming feeling of wanting to deliver his own children one day.

"Slow day in the baby ward today, so you stop by to check on me?" John asked, taking a sip of his drink.

"I wanted to ask how things were going with the purchase of the new building?"

We just met with the realtor last week. We haven't gotten a report back from the inspector or the appraiser. That could take a few months."

"Oh, I didn't know it would take that long before you could even bid on the property."

"This is a marathon, not a race. We cross every T and dot every I. But, I have a feeling you didn't really want to know about the progress of the building. I think you want to know more about the beautiful realtor that has gotten under your skin."

"Who said anything about getting under my skin? I'm just intrigued by her," Grant took a sip of the wine, looked at the glass, then drained the remaining contents. "I think I need something stronger than this."

"Yep, like I said, under your skin." John went to the minibar and poured himself and his brother a double-shot of Whiskey. "Listen, big brother, no need to be aggressive with this woman. She seems to be the type that is all about business first. Just chill and wait for the perfect opportunity."

"Well, I wish I could, but you don't know the half of things."

Grant told his brother about the day's earlier events, and the fact he had been working with Kyna for the past six months. John dropped his head and started laughing hysterically. "You, my brother, are in for a roller coaster ride. For once, I am glad I get a front-row seat to it all."

Chapter 3

Grant had the weekend off from being on call with the hospital, and he intended to get caught up on some medical journal readings, but his thoughts continued to linger back to Kaleigh. After his talk with his brother, Grant returned to his apartment by the hospital and stayed up most of the night thinking about ways to approach Kaleigh without being aggressive. He had to stop the urge he had to look her up or call Kyna to find out how she was doing. He was genuinely concerned about her.

Instead of hanging around his apartment on a Sunday morning, he decided to go to church. His attendance was mostly dependent upon his schedule at the hospital. Grant would typically attend the early service, just because the pastor would usually stay timely to the hour and a half service time. Grant had awakened late and decided not to rush and attend the later service.

The parking lot was unusually crowded. Upon entering, Grant greeted a few people he knew and stopped by the coffee bar, which was just two Keurigs and an array of flavored K-cups. Kevin, a young musician he met when his wife gave birth a few months ago, approached him.

"Hey, Dr. Hawkins, how are things?"

"Been good. How's the baby?"

"Healthy and loud. I wish someone had told me how loud babies get when they don't get their way," Kevin laughed at himself.

"So, what's going on today? I've missed a few weeks."

"Oh yeah, Eden Missionary Baptist Church is visiting today. They are installing their new pastor this evening. So, they are worshipping with us this morning, and we are going over there later. Hey, service is about to begin, let me go. It was good seeing you, Doc."

"Good seeing you too, Kevin."

Grant finished his coffee in the lobby before heading into the main sanctuary for service. His routine was to sit in the back, on the right side of the church, which was closest to the exit. Just in case he got a call to return to the hospital, his departure wouldn't be disruptive. Today was different, he didn't have his tethering device, also known as his on-call pager, and he was free to sit anywhere. Grant started down the middle aisle, looking for a place to sit when he spotted two familiar faces. Kyna and one of her sisters were sitting up front with a group of people he had not seen before. He figured they must all be members of Eden MBC.

Suddenly, Grant had a perfect idea. He remembered what his brother told him about being aggressive. Instead of directly asking Kaleigh on a date, he would ask her to do her job. Grant was in the market for a house and just hadn't gotten around to actually house-hunting. The timing was perfect, and this would force her to have to work with him side-by-side.

The deacons entered the sanctuary from a backroom, which indicated the service was beginning. Grant quickly took a seat next to Mrs. Henderson in the row where he was standing. She was a quiet, older woman in the church who rarely spoke to him or anyone else.

When Grant sat down, Mrs. Henderson patted his knee, gave him a quick smile, then focused her attention on the deacons. The small gesture warmed his heart.

Grant directed his attention in the vicinity of where the Hammond sisters were sitting. He hadn't seen Kaleigh or their other sister enter. Maybe they didn't attend the same church. Grant tried to listen to the church announcements but couldn't. His mind was still on wondering where Kaleigh was.

"Let us welcome the praise team from Eden," Pastor Martin said.

The beat of the drums started, and the band began to play. "Come on, church, put your hands together, and let's give the Lord some praise."

He knew that voice, and it had Grant jerking his head up quickly to see Kaleigh in the pulpit with the microphone in hand. Grant couldn't stop smiling. This woman amazed him at every turn. She was beautiful, intelligent, independent, and she could sing. If she surprised him one more time, he was sure Kaleigh Hammond would become Mrs. Hawkins.

For the following 20 minutes, Grant was awestruck watching Kaleigh lead praise and worship, and how her voice spoke right to him. She had a deep, sultry tone with a southern rasp. He wanted more and was disappointed when it was time for his pastor to deliver the word. Grant thought he could listen to her sing all day and night.

After service, Grant wanted to leave without sticking around to talk to some of the guys like he usually would. He didn't want the church mothers to see him. But, that plan was thwarted by Deaconess Greene, who stopped him to discuss having an informational session on women's health. Deaconess Greene could talk long, switch subjects without taking a breath, and it was difficult trying to get her to stop. Out of respect, Grant listened to her and responded accordingly.

"Oh, Dr. Hawkins, I want to introduce you to my sorority sister's daughter. She is a nurse at your hospital. She is right over here with her sisters." Deaconess had grabbed his hand and was dragging him across the lobby. Before he realized it, he was standing right in front of the Hammond sisters again.

"Kyna, this is the doctor I was telling you about." Mrs. Greene introduced him.

"Mrs. Greene, I know Dr. Hawkins quite well," Kyna smiled. "I work on his service."

"Oh, that is wonderful. I want you two to partner up for the women's day health initiative. The women in this church could use more information on being healthy." Deaconess Greene continued to talk, but Grant had tuned her out.

He couldn't believe how his luck, or lack thereof, kept putting him in front of Kaleigh. This was the third time within 7 days.

"Kaleigh, I see you are feeling better today," Grant asked.

"Much better after a full day's rest. Thank you for asking," Kaleigh responded, averting her eyes from connecting with his.

"My dear, were you sick?" Mrs. Greene asked.

"Nothing serious. If you will excuse me," Kaleigh turned and walked away toward the front doors.

Grant had to stop her. He needed to ask her about helping him find a house.

"Excuse me, Deaconess." He then rushed behind Kaleigh. "Kaleigh, can I talk with you for a moment?"

"I'm on my way to another appointment. Can you talk and walk?" she tossed over her shoulder as she quickly walked away.

*****

What was it with this guy? Why was he popping up everywhere she went? Kaleigh was just as shocked to see him in church as she was to see him at the restaurant. His presence was unnerving, and she was struggling to deal with the underlying attraction that she knew he felt at their first meeting.

"I wanted to talk to you about helping me to buy a house."

"From what I understand, Dr. Hawkins, you are only expected to be here temporarily."

"Well, I have changed my mind, and I've decided to stay for a while."

"Long enough to want to buy a house?" she asked. Kaleigh was well aware of the small-town charm and incorporated city life that has snagged quite a few visitors in recent years. The town was growing by leaps and bounds, and the good doctor was not immune to its captivating draw.

But, if he thought for one minute that having her help him look for a house was a way to get a date with her, he was sadly mistaken.

"Listen, Dr. Hawkins."

"Please, call me Grant," he stuffed his hands in his pants pockets and gave her his signature smile.

"Dr. Hawkins," Kaleigh insisted. "If this is some kind of half-hatched plan to get me to go on a date with you, then please look somewhere else. I haven't the time to play games."

"No games. I really did extend my contract with the hospital for ten years. I was planning to stay when my brother first mentioned he wanted to build a hotel here. I don't get to see my siblings much anymore. So, this is the perfect opportunity."

For a quick second, Kaleigh heard some sadness in his voice when he mentioned his siblings. She knew what it was like to be away from her sisters for an extended period. Her four years in college were difficult being away from home. She couldn't imagine not being within driving distance of her sisters.

"Okay. Call the office tomorrow and schedule an appointment with an available agent. I only hire the best, so you will get great service." They had reached her vehicle in the parking lot, and she reached for the door when Grant's hand stopped her.

"I don't want another agent. I only want to work with the best, and that is you."

"Dr. Hawkins…"

"Grant," he attempted to correct her.

Kaleigh rolled her eyes before continuing, "I am far too busy. My schedule is booked up for at least the next few weeks."

"I will wait then." He smiled and opened her car door. "Please drive safely."

Kaleigh gave him a death stare when he closed her door and walked away wearing that smug smile of his. She was not going to get caught up in his charm, no matter what he thought.

The next morning, Kaleigh walked into her office by 10 A.M. Her migraine from Saturday had hit her hard Sunday night, and she had a difficult time trying to get rid of it. She had grown tired of all of the medications that had been prescribed to her over the years. Not one single pill worked. She had resorted to creating her own concoctions to gain some type of relief.

The migraine was gone by morning, but she woke with lower back spasms. She opted to soak in her jacuzzi tub and took a muscle relaxer to ease the pain. By the time she was feeling better, it was past the time she would typically go to the gym before heading into the office. She texted Karmyn, who owned the gym where she worked out, so her sister wouldn't get concerned.

Any deviation from a well-set plan and Karmyn would think a sister had been kidnapped and sold.

"Good morning, Janice."

"Good morning, Ms. Hammond," she replied, handing Kaleigh the mail and a new client file. "We have a new client. He has been waiting for you since 9 A. M."

"Why didn't you get someone else to assist him?"

"He insisted on you and said he would wait."

Instantly, Kaleigh began feeling sick to her stomach. She was growing tired of Dr. Hawkins, and it had only been a week since they first met.

"Where is he?"

"In the conference room," Janice said, smiling.

Kaleigh went to her office first. She would make him wait a little longer. How dare he just show up to her office without an appointment? She told him to call, and apparently, he didn't listen very well. After getting comfortable and reviewing his intake profile, she took her time making coffee before going to the conference room.

"Dr. Hawkins, I asked you to call. I told you I am swamped."

"I thought it would be easier for me to drop by and make my appointment. Your receptionist said you didn't have any appointments until this afternoon, so I decided to wait for you. She also said you usually arrive by 8:30 A. M. Are you feeling okay today?"

Kaleigh took a seat in the chair across from Grant. She took two calming breaths before staring him in the eyes. "Dr. Grant, listen very carefully. I am not interested in you. Even if I were, your reputation precedes you. Also, you work with my sister. Please believe I have heard stories, and I am sure those are the clean versions. So please understand, if you want to find your forever home, my associates are more than competent."

Grant looked down, shook his head, and then raised his eyes to meet hers. "If you insist. I'll work with another agent." He stood, nodded his head to her, and left the conference room.

Kaleigh collapsed in her chair as the door closed. She didn't understand how one man, whom she just met, could cause her to have the type of inner turmoil she was having. She wanted to concentrate on his brother's major deal and not on anything else, including him.

The door to the conference room opened and in walked Janice and Regina. Regina joined the agency last year and had been the top realtor 7 out of the previous 12 months. Her sales numbers were crucial for keeping K. Hammond Realty afloat.

"Sooo. Tell us. What did Dr. So Fine want?" Regina asked like a high school teenager.

"Seriously, you two. He wants to buy a house. I'm thinking about giving him to Carl."

"Carl!" Janice and Regina said in unison.

"You've got to be kidding me. You want to put Carl on a potential million-dollar sale."

"Where did you get a million dollars from?" Kaleigh asked.

"You didn't read his profile, did you? He's looking for a home on the lake, at least 4,500 square feet. As far as I know, that house only exists in the million-dollar range."

Kaleigh thought about that bit of information for a minute before responding. "Perfect. Carl will be perfect." Kaleigh stood to leave the room. "Janice, give his profile to Carl and make sure I'm not disturbed until lunch.

The two women looked at Kaleigh incredulously before leaving the room.

Kaleigh spent the next few hours reviewing the appraisals of the two buildings that The Hawkins Group was interested in. Building 1 had some structural issues. The extent of damage and repair was undetermined at the time. Building 2 came back slightly more expensive than the initial purchase price. The historic preservation report returned that the building was on a list to be determined if it was a historical landmark. That could be good and bad.

If it is deemed a historical landmark, the building would be more valuable and would be subject to strict restoration codes. If the building was not a historical site, they could offer a lower bid. Reviewing the financials and documents of each building was straining on Kaleigh's eyes. She needed to look away and look at something pretty and not stressful. Closing her eyes, she tried to imagine tulips and puppies but was only coming up with old buildings and cracking facades.

There was a knock on her office door bringing back to the present. Kaleigh opened her eyes and silently prayed away her oncoming migraine.

"Yes, come in."

Janice walked into the office and placed a huge bouquet of white roses in a beautiful glass vase on her side table. Without saying a word, she backed out of the office wearing a huge grin. Kaleigh didn't get a chance to read the card that came with the flowers because her phone started ringing. The ringtone for Kyna blared from her mobile phone.

"Yes, Sister, how may I help you?"

"Stop it with the office voice. What did you do to Dr. Hawkins?"

Kaleigh's migraine was intensifying with the sound of his name. "What do you mean, what did I do to him? I did nothing to him."

"Okay, then what did you say to him? He came to work with a huge smile on his face and humming a tune. I have never seen him do that. I know he came to see you this morning."

Kyna's tone was more accusatory than gentle questioning. Kaleigh stood to smell her roses before answering her sister. Often, Kaleigh found it hard to believe she was the older sister. "How do you know that?"

"Because I heard him telling another doctor he was looking for a house. When that doctor told him about his realtor, he said, and I quote, 'I'm already working with the best realtor in town at K. Hammond Realty.' Seriously, Sister, the man has the hots for you. Just don't turn into one of these women that are always calling the hospital."

"I have done nothing to the good doctor. And trust me, I will not be calling after or running behind any man." Kaleigh tried to say it with conviction, yet she didn't believe it herself.

Kyna laughed and ended the call with no further words. Kaleigh dropped her head into her hands and then began laughing at herself. The whole situation was comical to her. Men have asked her on dates before, but typically took the hint when she didn't entertain their advances. None of them had ever stooped so low as to purchase a home to get her attention.

*****

Grant was impressed that Kaleigh held to her guns about not working with him as his realtor. The agent she assigned to him was a bit slow for his taste. The guy didn't return calls in what Grant deemed an appropriate amount of time. He was sure with the right persuasion; Carl would help him with his mission. And that mission was to get Kaleigh on one date.

Carl was scheduled to meet him at a house located on Georgetown Lake. The fact sheet showed the house had everything he was looking for, including a swimming pool with an attached hot tub. He couldn't wait to see the inside, but Carl was 15 minutes late. Punctuality was something Grant felt strongly about.

While he waited, Grant called his brother, Morgan. He wanted to know how things were going with the building purchase.

"Grant, this is a special occasion. You rarely call me. I know there is nothing wrong with John, and Melissa is with me. Are you okay?"

"Ever the perceptive, Brother. I just called to see how things are coming along with your new acquisition."

"You have never once been interested in what we do here, so this must have to do with Ms. Hammond," Morgan laughed.

"I don't even know why I called you," Grant silently admonished himself.

'Yes, you do. You called because you need someone in your corner, someone to be on your side as you pursue her. Unfortunately, we cannot help you. It would be very unethical. Wouldn't you say so, Dr. Hawkins?"

"I hate it when you draw the self-righteous, big brother card. Don't worry, I'll find other allies." Grant ended the call as a black sedan pulled up behind him.

Finally, he thought.

"I'm sorry, Dr. Hawkins, the hot sign at the donut shop was on, and I couldn't resist."

Unbelievable! This guy was late for an appointment because he stopped for fresh donuts. Grant could not believe Kaleigh would have someone so careless in her employment.

"Mr. Atwater, I find it highly unacceptable that you would have a client waiting because you wanted donuts."

"You're right, Dr. Hawkins, but I just can't resist that hot sign." Carl dismissed Grant and continued. "Let's go inside, shall we?"

Carl talked incessantly while Grant walked around the home. He was impressed that Carl seemed to know the housing business. The house was near perfect…only one problem. He really wanted one person's opinion.

"Mr. Atwater?"

"Please, call me Carl. I'm sorry I've been talking a lot. I have found that clients have lots of questions, and I like to answer them before they are asked."

"You have been very thorough with your knowledge of the house. How many other homes do you have for me to view?"

"You want to see more? This one checks every box you had on your wish list. Geez, what more do you want?"

That was it, Grant had had it with Carl. Instead of responding to his complaint, he decided to just walk away. Anything Grant said would come out the wrong way. Grant left Carl, still standing in the kitchen, slack-jawed and stunned that he had walked away.

Before Grant arrived at the hospital, his phone was ringing.

"Dr. Hawkins, this is Kaleigh Hammond. I am calling to apologize to you for Carl's behavior today."

"How do you know what happened?"

"Carl called to complain and requested that another agent be assigned to you. I'm sure it was nothing you did, so I can only assume Carl rubbed you the wrong way."

"The guy who was late by 20 minutes, talked non-stop, and then became enraged because I wanted to see other homes, actually called to complain about me?"

"Again, Dr. Hawkins, I am so sorry about this. This will not happen again."

"You got that right. I want to work with only you."

There was a pause, and Grant figured she was trying to think of a way to get out of working with him. Before she could object, Grant jumped in, "Kaleigh, I don't bite…okay? I am seriously looking for a house, and I would like you to work with me. My brother John said you are close to negotiating a deal on one of the properties, so I can wait until then."

"Thank you, Dr. Hawkins. I will have Janice schedule some viewings with you in the next few weeks."

"I look forward to hearing from her." Grant ended the call with an enormous smile on his face. Things were falling into place like divine order. He couldn't have planned this any better.

Whistling a tune, with a kick in his step, Grant entered the hospital and went straight to his office. Kyna saw him on his way in, and she gave him an all-knowing look. He needed to get her on his side. That would be a challenge.

Grant couldn't remember having to work this hard for a date, but somehow, he knew it would be all worth it in the end.

Chapter 4

"This house was built in 2010 by NBA player George Falls. He installed a deck from the lower level that leads to a boat dock on the back of the house," Kaleigh continued to describe the house to Grant while they walked from room to room.

As long as she was talking about the house, she wouldn't mistakenly say something she didn't want to. Being this close to Grant was causing her senses to go in overdrive. He was his usual handsome self, wearing a custom-tailored suit with diamond-encrusted cufflinks. His clean-shaven face gave him a boyish appearance, but it was the intensity in his deep chocolate eyes that caused her knees to buckle.

"Kaleigh, I really like this house. What do you think about it?"

"I think if you like it, I love it."

"Could you imagine living here yourself, raising a family in a house like this?"

"I don't know. It's a little too opulent for my style. I guess if I could afford it, I may be convinced to enjoy living here."

Grant was quietly observing her. As she talked, she became softer and let her business wall crumble a little. He could tell she enjoyed her job but enjoyed it more when she could fantasize about living in the homes she viewed.

"Am I talking too much?"

"No, I was just noticing how you relaxed when you talked about living here."

"Oh, I didn't realize." Kaleigh tried to return to her business-like manner and continue with the tour. She didn't mean to drop her guard around him. She continued to show him around the house and point out special features and additions. By the end of the tour, Kaleigh was getting anxious to get away from Grant. He was too much, too soon.

"If you like, we can put in an offer today. The list price is $1.7 million, but I think we should offer $1.4 million. There is a little updating that would need to be done."

"I don't think I am ready to make a hasty decision. How many more houses can we view?"

"Somehow, Dr. Hawkins, I believe you may be dragging this out or not truly interested in purchasing a home."

"I can assure you that I am serious about purchasing. It just needs to be perfect, and I am not getting perfect vibes from this one."

"Fine. There is another house, just down the road. I will contact the listing agent and make an appointment."

"Kaleigh, can we meet for coffee one day this week? I would like to talk to you on a more social level."

"Dr. Hawkins, the flowers were nice, but as I have said before, I am not interested."

"You can't fault a man for trying."

"If nothing at all, you are persistent. I will have Janice call you to schedule your next viewing. Have a nice day."

Kaleigh returned the key to the lockbox outside of the house and moved toward her car. She had an uneasy, nauseated feeling overcome her. Each step felt slower and sluggish, and she tried hard to keep moving one step in front of the other. Along with the nausea were dizziness and confusion. Kaleigh struggled to reach her car. The area around her appeared in slow motion, and the only thing she could do was pray not to faint again.

Finally making it to her car, she found her key fob, unlocked the door, and entered. For several minutes she sat behind the steering wheel, trying to regain her senses. Kaleigh hoped that Grant had left and was not a witness to her craziness, again. She took several deep breaths before starting the car.

Water! She needed water. She managed to squeeze her body between the middle console and reach in the back seat for a bottle of water. The water would be warmer than room temperature, but that didn't matter; she just hoped that it would do the trick. Kaleigh took a few swigs of the warm liquid and let it soothe her internally. She waited a few more minutes to see if the water and the cool breeze from the car's air-conditioner would clear up her head fog.

Kaleigh didn't know what came over her. She needed to keep a record of the random things that had begun happening to her. After sitting in her vehicle with the air-conditioning running on full blast, she finally started feeling like herself. The air was working to calm her senses.

Instead of returning to her office, Kaleigh went straight home to rest. Later in the evening, she would be attending a fundraiser with her sisters that would benefit an organization that Karleigh and her fiancé Simon Sharpe had started. Simon Sharpe was the owner of the Sharper Image Barber Shops.

Stay Sharp was an organization that provided entrepreneurial mentoring to teenagers. The couple created a co-working shared space where youth as young as 13 could come and benefit from courses, one-on-one business coaching, and networking with other entrepreneurs in the community.

The gala was a fundraiser to raise money to open another co-working space on the other side of town. Simon had high-end clients, including professional athletes and C-suite executives, who were always willing to give to a worthy cause. Simon's best friend Nick Butler was an attorney for the elite and added his clientele to the already star-studded event.

Kaleigh didn't need much time to prepare and dress for the evening. Her dress was already selected, and she didn't wear much makeup. Her hair was short and styled very easily. Instead of primping in a mirror, Kaleigh decided to take a nap. She turned her phone off and pulled the shades in her bedroom closed. A good three hours of rest should do the trick.

"She can't be asleep; she knows how much this evening means to Karleigh and Simon," Kyna said to Karmyn as they arrived at Kaleigh's house.

"Her car is outside, so she must be here." Karmyn used the spare key given to her in case of an emergency to open the door and enter.

"Poe! Poe, are you here?" Kyna yelled through the house. Karmyn started heading toward her bedroom.

Kaleigh heard the voices but thought they were in her dreams. She felt like she had only been asleep a few minutes. Rolling to her side, Poe forced her eyes open to see the clock on her nightstand. She blinked a couple times to bring the bold red numbers into focus. Finally, comprehending that she had not been asleep for just a few minutes, Poe jumped when Karmyn barged into her bedroom.

"Poe, are you in here?" Karmyn asked. "Oh, my God. Poe get up. You overslept."

She jumped from the bed and raced into the bathroom. "I'm so sorry! I promise I set the alarm clock. I can be ready in 20 minutes."

She couldn't believe she had slept through the alarm clock. That had never happened before. Her migraines and lack of sleep lately must have been the cause of her having slept so heavy.

Poe took 10 minutes to stop her racing heart and control her breathing from being scared awake. She splashed water on her face and applied a moisturizer to her skin. Her dress was on a hanger in her closet, along with her jewelry and shoes. Twenty-five minutes later, Poe was dressed and ready to go.

"Speedy Gonzales in there. It took me almost 2 hours to get dressed," Kyna responded when Poe finally exited her bedroom.

Poe had selected a full-length Gold sheath gown. The dress had a plunging neckline, and the side split stopped mid-thigh on Poe. She felt sexy and alluring in this dress. Far from her business attire and work-out gear, that was the majority of her wardrobe.

"I don't wear nearly as much make-up as you do. Besides, you probably went through several different dresses before you settled on one," Poe teased her sister.

"You know your sister well. She tried on 17 dresses and settled on three," Karmyn stated. Kyna was wearing a designer original from the House of Honey, a friend of Kyna's from high school. The dress was a mini-skirt in the front and had a cape tail that dragged the floor even in Kyna's four-inch heels.

"What do you mean settled on three?" Poe asked.

"She has the other two in the car. She is planning a wardrobe change mid-way through the gala." Karmyn responded to her sister, rolling her eyes at the diva antics Kyna was known for. Karmyn's dress was a classic black strapless dress with a ruffled, feathered bottom. She always wanted others to see her physique. Showing off her muscular toned arms was good publicity for her gym and her personal training sessions.

"You all will not talk about me like I'm not sitting right here," Kyna whined. In a huff, she grabbed her designer handbag from the table. "Can we leave now? We're already going to be late. Karleigh is going to kill us."

Karmyn and Poe both laughed at their sister before leaving the house. Kyna was known for drama, and the sisters allowed it because she was the youngest.

The ballroom of the JW Hotel was in full swing as the three sisters entered. Karleigh and Simon had outdone themselves, putting this event together. There were dozens of white and red roses all over the ballroom, and each table's centerpiece was decorated with beautiful arrangements of red and white flowers. They arrived at the end of the cocktail hour and were escorted to their assigned tables for dinner by a couple of the youth from the Stay Sharp program who were serving as hosts.

Karleigh had seen them enter late and cut her eyes at them briefly before returning to the conversation she was having with a potential donor. Poe was sure they would hear about her disappointment at their late arrival before the night was over. This was the first joint event for Karleigh and Simon, and Karleigh wanted everything to be perfect. By the looks of the room and everyone in attendance, Karleigh had nothing to worry about.

The sisters were escorted to a front table near the dance floor. They had a great view of the entire ballroom. Also seated at their table were Simon's best friend Nick and two stylists, Echo and Whisper, from Karleigh's salon. Poe didn't know what Karleigh was thinking by putting Nick and Karmyn at the same table. The two of them could barely stand the presence of one another, and both kept quiet as to why.

Poe was feeling much better than she had earlier in the day. She was still a little tired but felt good and decided to truly enjoy herself for the evening. It was past time that she relax and just enjoy life. After dinner, there would be a short presentation and then a pledge for donations before the dancing began. Poe couldn't wait for the band to play; she felt like dancing the night away. The program was short and sweet, a few acknowledgments, and "thank you's" to their donors and those who donated on the spot, then the band started up.

*****

Grant must have the best of luck. He couldn't believe his eyes when he saw her enter the ballroom. She was dazzling in a floor-length gold dress that hugged every curve, even curves he didn't know she had. The split gave him just enough of a view to see her well-toned thigh. He guessed she worked out with her sister at her gym. Kaleigh gracefully walked across the room, stopping to greet people here and there. Her smile was radiant. She wore minimal make-up, and he was glad for it. She didn't do much to her hair either, except for adding a jeweled clip to the side.

He must have sat there, staring at her for 15 minutes. Just marveling in her beauty. Grant had an overwhelming need to just be close to her.

"Yep, you've got it bad. I hope I don't catch what you have," John laughed.

"I don't even know her well enough to have it this bad," Grant responded to his brother's bad attempt at a joke.

"You remember what Dad said about meeting Mom. He knew the first time he saw her, she would be his wife. And, they had never talked to one another."

Grant thought about the stories their parents told them about how they met, fell in love, and eventually married. They were about to celebrate their 40th wedding anniversary. His father must know something about finding a wife. Grant shook his head and laughed at himself. Why in the world was he thinking about finding a wife?

Grant was attending the gala as his brother's plus one. After the house showing earlier in the day, Grant had planned to spend his evening alone in thought of how to get Kaleigh to at least have coffee with him. Instead, his brother forced him into a suit and dragged him to the gala.

The Hawkins Group was frequently invited to fundraising events around the country. John needed to attend as many events locally as he could. The Hawkins family needed to build as many relationships as possible in the community if they intended to do business there.

Grant believed it to be no coincidence that he and his brother were seated with the president of the city council, several other members of the council, and the deputy mayor. John had his ways of making connections and tossing his name and money around to get what he wanted.

The event was proving to be a typical community fundraiser. A few women Grant had dated, and some who had tried to date him were in attendance. He noticed quite a few other women smiling in his direction. One woman he didn't know wanted to attach herself to him by following him around the ballroom. Grant was finally able to shake her when she went to touch-up her makeup.

He was getting tired of being there at, yet, another $100 a plate dinner. Grant was about to tell his brother good night for the evening; he was not going to make it through dinner. Before he could interrupt his brother, who was speaking with some city officials, Kaleigh entered with her sisters.

Grant was now on alert and listening to every conversation around him, waiting for an opportunity or an opening that would help him with Kaleigh. He was currently sitting 5 tables behind her and her sisters. Formulating a plan on short notice was not working. His brain was in a fog, and he was openly staring at her. Councilwoman Deborah Jackson reached over the table and touched his hand, breaking his concentration.

"Dr. Hawkins, if you need an introduction, I will gladly provide one. It is very obvious you are interested in one of the Hammond sisters."

"Am I that open?" Grant tried to laugh, but the councilwoman was not swayed.

"You haven't taken your eyes from their table since they've been seated. They are beautiful girls."

Yes, they were, but it was only one sister that Grant was interested in. He returned the councilwoman's smile and said, "I think I can handle it, but thank you."

Grant didn't leave and decided to stay for the dinner and the presentations. Afterward, the band began to play, and the dance floor filled within minutes. Grant took this as his opportunity to approach Kaleigh. He made his way toward her table and stopped short. She was sitting comfortably close to a man who had his arm draped around her shoulders.

His immediate gut reaction was to forcibly remove this man from touching his woman. Then, he had to think again; because, first, she wasn't his woman…yet. Second, he had no reason to feel jealous. It was an emotion he was unfamiliar with. Yet, there he was staring at a woman, grinding his teeth.

"You know, the smoke coming from your ears is visible."

Attempting to regain his composure, he replied, "Nurse Kyna, how are you?"

"Let's cut the chit-chat, Grant," she said with an attitude. "If your intentions are honorable, then I'll help you, but you have to do something for this help."

"Go ahead…continue."

"I am not your personal secretary. I will no longer field calls for your many admirers…that is to include nurses, doctors, and other liaisons. Listen…" She paused for dramatic effect. "I know you are not the playboy doctor that you pretend to be. My friend Georgia went out with you a few months ago, and you barely engaged with her. She's beautiful and intelligent, yet, you didn't even take her up on her offer of a post-dinner nightcap." Kyna smiled at a couple who passed by them. She waited before she continued. "Poe is complicated. You have to come correct with her."

"Who is Poe?" Grant asked, confused.

"It's a name we call her. She can tell you why, *if* she wants to." Kyna turned to fully face the doctor and extended her hand to him. "Do we have a deal?"

Grant stared at his nurse, the most competent person on his service. She was small, but feisty, smart, and didn't back down from a challenge. Not in the hospital and not here. He decided to accept her help.

"Deal." he took her hand in his much larger one, and they shook on it.

Grant watched the man with Kaleigh move away from her and closer to another woman at their table. He hadn't noticed he was clenching his jaw until Kyna spoke again.

"He is nothing to worry about. Go ahead, make your move now. Ask her about The Raven," Kyna said before walking away toward the dance floor.

Grant had no idea what Kyna was talking about, but he wasn't stupid, either. He made his way toward her table and, again, stopped short. He could smell her fragrance, and he wanted to take in her scent and sight just once more before approaching.

"Is this seat taken?" Grant asked, standing directly behind Kaleigh.

She glanced up and smiled before realizing who it was. Immediately her smiled faltered.

"Are you following me?" Kaleigh asked. Grant noticed her voice wasn't laced with venom and accepted that she wasn't upset.

"Not at all, I like to call it fate or destiny," Grant pulled out the chair to her left and took a seat. He noticed how her breathing picked up, and she wouldn't look him straight in the eyes. She kept her gaze on the dance floor.

"Well, I call it very suspect and stalker-ish," Kaleigh responded.

Grant opened his mouth to say something but was interrupted. "Hey, Dr. Hawkins! Fancy seeing you here," Karmyn said, returning to her seat on the other side of Kaleigh.

"Karmyn, right?" Grant asked, knowing exactly which sister she was.

"That's me," Karmyn smiled and gave a noticeable wink to her sister. Kaleigh rolled her eyes and made an unladylike snort. She then stood from the table and attempted to walk away.

"Hey, where are you going?" Grant gently grabbed Kaleigh's hand as she stood. He needed to hold on to the opportunity for as long as he could.

"I'm going to find a drink," Kaleigh said with a tinge of irritation in her voice.

"How about I join you?" Without releasing her hand, he stood, tucked her hand into the curve of his elbow, and walked with her toward the bar. Grant smiled and inwardly congratulated himself because she hadn't pulled away from him.

Halfway to the bar, the woman Grant tried to hide from earlier in the evening blocked their path. "Grant, I thought you were here alone," she pouted.

Grant thought the woman wore too much makeup, and she appeared to be a little drunk. Both made her unattractive to him. Before Grant could correct the woman, he felt Kaleigh remove her hand and step away from him.

"I'm not here with Grant. You are free to entertain him all night." Kaleigh then turned to Grant and said, "Goodnight," before quickly excusing herself in the opposite direction.

Grant couldn't stop Kaleigh from leaving because the lady with too much makeup jumped up and threw her arms around his neck. The smell of her perfume and alcohol mixed caused Grant to feel slightly nauseous. It took some doing, but he was able to effectively evade her attempts to kiss him. Grant couldn't believe the audacity of this woman. Many women had made plays for him, but none like this.

After passing the woman off to security, he went in search of Kaleigh. Kyna used her eyes to point him in the direction that Kaleigh went. He found her sitting in the garden area of the hotel.

She was a stunning vision, simply beautiful, surrounded by flowers. For several minutes, Grant just watched her. He didn't want to interrupt her alone time, but he wanted so much just to be near her.

"So, there are you," Grant said, finally approaching her.

"Had enough of the walking Revlon counter," Kaleigh rolled her eyes.

Was that jealousy he heard in her voice? He shook his head because he must have been hearing things.

"She was drunk. Besides, she's not my type."

"What is your type, Dr. Hawkins?" Kaleigh asked, turning toward him as he sat next to her on the bench.

"Well, I prefer an intelligent woman. One who is independent doesn't need a man to make her who she is. I prefer a Christian woman with good values. I like a woman with her own identity and not the one looking to be the next Mrs. Dr. Grant."

"Is that all? What about looks?"

"That type of woman is always beautiful…" Grant smiled at Kaleigh's reaction. Her eyes lit up like billboards on time square. "But, beauty is in the eye of the beholder. I prefer natural beauty; a woman who doesn't need much to enhance what God blessed her with."

When she didn't have a quick retort, Grant moved a little closer to her and was about to ask her on a date again. Instead, he was interrupted by the guy who had been sitting at her table.

"Poe, are you ready to get out of here?" Nick asked her without acknowledging Grant.

"Yes. Let me grab my shawl from the table. Nick, do you know Dr. Hawkins?"

Grant stood to greet Nicolas, "Dr. Grant Hawkins, nice to meet you."

Nicolas accepted his hand, "Nicolas Butler, it's a pleasure." Then turning back to Poe, Nick said, "I will get your shawl and meet you in the front.

Grant watched their dry interaction and determined that Kaleigh and Mr. Butler were not romantically involved. The green-eyed monster of jealousy returned to his place, deep undercover.

"Dr. Hawkins, have a good evening," Kaleigh said, leaving Grant alone in the garden.

Under his breath, Grant murmured, "it's not over Ms. Hammond."

Chapter 5

The next morning, after the gala, Poe awakened with a penetrating migraine headache. She was unable to open her eyes as she stumbled her way from the bedroom into the adjoining bathroom. With eyes still closed, she managed to find the sink and face cloth. The wet, cool cloth across her temples wasn't working to ease the pain. She fumbled around in her medicine cabinet, trying to find some aspirin. Each time she opened her eyes, she felt dizzy and had to immediately close them again.

She wished she had listened to her mother about putting curtains in the bathroom. If she had curtains, she would be able to block out the sunlight filtering through the windows. After several attempts, she found the aspirin and inhaled four capsules. Collapsing against the tiled floor and waiting for the medicine to take effect. If she had her way, the floor would swallow her whole and take the pain away.

Poe felt like she had been on the floor for hours, only to realize it had been 45 minutes. She managed to open her eyes enough to crawl back to the comfort of her bed and the darkness. She didn't care if it was a Sunday; there was no way she was leaving her house. She would just have to miss church, and Ms. Byrd would have to adjust the music ministry. Even if she could make it to church, there was no way she was singing.

Sundays were also family time. The sisters would join their parents and their paternal grandmother at church in the morning, then afterward, have dinner at their parents' house. Her mother was the best cook in the city, and she always put together a spread of food.

The mere thought of food had Poe's stomach churning. She was trying to remember what she ate or drank the night before, but just thinking caused her head to pound harder and faster. She had never felt like this; the pounding was like someone hitting her over the head with a bat. She couldn't open her eyes without it feeling like an explosion in her brain, and her stomach flipped and flopped like an Olympic gymnast. Then, she felt bile rising in her throat. Without thinking, she raced to her bathroom and dry-heaved over the toilet.

One thing Poe could rule out for sure... she wasn't pregnant. But, trying to think of another cause had her laid out on the floor, writhing in pain. That was just how Karleigh found her. When Poe didn't answer her phone or the door, Karleigh let herself in using her spare key and found Poe on the floor of the bathroom in pain.

"Sister! Oh, my God! What's wrong? I'm calling 911."

"No!" Poe whispered, but it sounded like shouting in her own ears. "It's just a headache."

"This is something more than a headache. At least let me call Kyna," Karleigh pleaded with her.

"Yeah, call her," Poe winced as the pounding in her head continued.

A few hours later, all four sisters sat around Poe's living room, silently looking from one to the other. None of them had gone to church, which was rare for them. Karmyn had sent their parents a text message, letting them know what was going on. Their parents and grandmother understood their need to take care of one another and didn't question their absence in church or at dinner.

By this time, Poe's headache had subsided tremendously but had yet to completely dissipate. She had a cool cloth on her forehead at Karmyn's insistence. Kyna made her drink several glasses of water over the last few hours. They also tried to get her to eat, but her stomach was still doing summersaults.

Tired of the silence, Poe slowly tried to open her eyes and looked at her sisters. Karleigh was reading a magazine, Karmyn was snuggled into the corner of the sofa, nodding off. Kyna was sitting in the kitchen, playing on her cell phone.

The love they had for one another was thick in the room, and Poe became emotional and started sobbing. She tried to cover it up by returning the cloth to her eyes, but Karleigh had seen her.

"Poe, what's wrong? Is the headache getting worse?" Karleigh asked in a quiet voice.

"I think we should get her to the hospital," Karmyn added, also whispering.

"I don't need a hospital. I'll be fine. I'm just hungry," Poe lied to her sisters. "I know you are, too. I can hear someone's stomach growling."

Kyna smiled and lowered her head. "That would be mine. I hadn't eaten breakfast yet when Karleigh called."

"I think we all need to eat. But, just the thought of food is turning my stomach. So, whatever y'all order, get me a side salad or some soup," Poe said.

Kyna had been texting their mother and had just received a message back that she would be bringing Sunday dinner to Poe's house. Their dad and grandmother would stay behind.

"I think we need to address the elephant in the room." Kyna turned to Poe, then to her other sisters. "Poe, you have been sick for a while. First, it was the sudden allergies a few years ago, then you passed out at the restaurant, now these migraines. I'm talking to you as a medical professional; you need to see your doctor."

Poe knew what her sister was saying was true. What Kyna didn't know was that she had been to the doctor several times over the past year, and they were not able to find anything wrong with her. Test after test only revealed that they were just as clueless now as they had been in the last year.

She was tired of being poked and prodded, only to be given more medications and sent on her way. Poe didn't want to say it in front of Kyna, but the healthcare system was a racket and scam.

Telling her sisters about her healthcare woes now would cause two things to happen. One, they would know her entire medical history; and two, they would also make it their personal mission to diagnose her with something—especially Kyna, since she was a nurse.

Poe didn't have a choice; she didn't keep secrets from her sisters, and she didn't want to start now. With a great deal of pain, she sat upright on the sofa and removed the cloth from her eyes. She noticed that someone had drawn the drapes to make it dark in the room, and she was forever grateful for that.

"I'm going to take some more aspirin and wait for Mom to get here with the food. Then, I'll share everything with you. Just know, I have seen a doctor."

Kyra arrived with several Tupperware containers of food. There was enough to feed a small village. Even after Kevin and Simon ate, there was still plenty of food. Not wanting to learn what was going on with her daughter second-hand, Kyra stayed to listen to Poe talk about everything she had been through for the past year.

"I have had MRI's, scans, blood tests, and all of it comes back within a normal range. The migraines just started within the last few months, but the asthma and breathing issues started last year. I have only passed out the one time at the restaurant," Poe explained.

"Well, I, for one, do not think they are doing enough," Kyra exclaimed.

The sisters smiled at her declaration. She was a mama bear, and her claws were beginning to show. She would stick-up and stand-by her daughters through anything.

"Kyna, you're sitting over there quiet. You're the medical professional, what are your thoughts?" Karleigh asked her.

Before Kyna answered, Poe had a deep feeling of despair. She wasn't sure she wanted to hear what her sister had to say. Kyna is known to give you the facts without thinking of how she delivers the message.

"I feel like you are doing all of the right things. This migraine scares me, and I might ask for another CT scan. Let's rule out any brain issues."

"I promise to do that tomorrow."

The room grew quiet again, and everyone just looked from one to the other. No one knew what to do, and crying wasn't going to help. After several minutes, Poe had to break the silence.

"Okay, Mom…sisters…you have to leave now. My headache is just a dull ache. I ate my food, and I feel much better right now. We all have to prepare for work in the morning."

"Well, I guess we are being kicked out," Kyna joked.

"I know when I am not wanted," Karmyn smiled and stood to stretch.

"I'll check on you tomorrow. Don't wake early, just get up when you are ready, promise me?" Karleigh asked her.

"I promise. I promise to keep everyone updated. I love you guys so much." Poe let a tear slip when her sisters and mother circled around her to hug her, but she knew it wouldn't end there. Her mother immediately went into prayer. By "Amen," all the women were reaching for tissues and dabbing their eyes.

*****

Dr. Hawkins was finishing a workout in Triumphant Fitness and Health Spa when Karmyn entered her gym. Grant was hopeful she wouldn't find it strange to see him there. He had, in fact, purchased a membership the week before meeting Kaleigh. The timing of his membership and his obvious interest in her sister could be taken the wrong way.

Truthfully, he had heard good things about her gym and had wanted to check things out a few months ago. Grant's schedule at the hospital and being on-call worked against him. Now, having more time available, he was beginning to make time for himself.

Seeing Kaleigh over-worked, stressed, and sick spoke to him; and his stressful schedule and his blood pressure were also indicators that he needed to slow down. He had his vital signs checked a few weeks ago, and they were a little on the high side. Not enough for medication or intervention, but enough to be proactive.

The hospital agreed to contract another gynecologist to assist him and provided funding for him to hire a physician's assistant.

With help, Grant would now have the time to do other things, like enjoy his new home and a certain beautiful woman.

"Hey, Dr. Hawkins, fancy seeing you here." Karmyn slung a backpack over her shoulder and scanned Grant up and down, clearly checking him out. He would have enjoyed the obvious assessment of his physique had her sister been the one to check him out like that.

"Hey, Karmyn. Nice gym, you have here." Grant grabbed his towel from the bar next to him and wiped the sweat from across his face.

"I like it. When did you become a member? I haven't seen you in here before."

"I came in last week and decided it was time I started taking better care of myself."

"Really!? And you expect me to believe that? I think you are trying to get to Poe and are using her sisters to glean any information you can."

Ignoring her questioning gaze and the partially truthful statement she just made, Grant asked her the one question that had been burning his brain since the gala. "Why do you call her Poe?"

"You don't know?" she laughed.

"You are the second person I have heard call her, Poe."

"Well, short story…she loves Edgar Allen Poe. She will have to tell you the rest." Karmyn stared at Grant, making him feel slightly uncomfortable. "You won't get any help from me, but I wish you luck; you're going to need it." Then, she stepped into his personal space, causing him to take a step back. She may be small, but she exuded strength. "And remember this, Doctor…Mess with my sister, cause her any undue pain, you will have to deal with me. And, I know people. You understand?" She walked away, leaving Grant unsure if he wanted to laugh or run.

He wasn't going to let Karmyn scare him away. Even her sisters knew Kaleigh was going to be difficult. Well, Grant liked challenges; and getting Kaleigh to go on one date was the first hurdle to jump. He was packing up his gym bag when he was paged to the hospital. And like the sudden disturbance of his pager, a thought suddenly jumped into his mind. Grant was looking forward to another eventful day in the hospital with patients and working on his plan for Kaleigh.

Grant made his way to the hospital in record time. He was entering just as his patient was arriving in the emergency room. She had been undergoing fertility treatments for over five years. And today, she would finally give birth to triplets. She was only 32 weeks into this pregnancy, but they knew from the beginning, it would be risky.

"Hello, Mrs. McCarter, how are you feeling?"

She answered between breaths, "I'm…okay…but…he's…not." She pointed to her husband, who looked like he was confused as to where he was.

"Mr. McCarter, are you okay?" Grant asked.

"I can't remember where I parked the car." He looked to his wife. "Did I park in the lot, or did I leave the car at the door?" Checking the pockets of his pants and jacket, he said, "I can't find the keys. What did I do with the keys?"

"Honey…you…left the…car…at the valet," Mrs. McCarter responded through labored breath.

Grant inwardly laughed at the couple. The birth of the first child always caused new parents to do and say crazy things. He was sure that the McCarters were not ready to have three babies. At every appointment with the two, Mr. McCarter would look slightly dizzy from the information. Then, seeing him now, Grant figured he was going to have to treat Mr. McCarter for anxiety.

"Well, let's get you back to delivery and prepare to welcome your babies into the world."

The McCarter's were taken to labor and delivery, and Dr. Hawkins went to find his team to prepare for their birth. The neonatal team was on standby. During the last ultrasound, at least one of the babies was much smaller than the other two. Grant wanted to be prepared for anything that could happen. The McCarter's had been waiting for years for this moment.

Robert McCarter was a music producer, and his wife, Renee, was a jazz singer when they met. Since then, they had been making beautiful music together. Suddenly, Grant imagined seeing Kaleigh pregnant with their child. He immediately shook his head to get rid of the thought, but it still lingered. He was sure she would be the most gorgeous pregnant woman he had ever seen.

"Dr. Hawkins? What is that goofy smile for?" Kyna asked as she walked into the delivery room.

"I'm just excited for the McCarter's."

"Well, if anyone deserves this blessing, they surely do."

Grant agreed. "Nurse Kyna, let's go deliver some blessings."

In less than 5 hours, the McCarter's delivered three small and healthy baby girls. Robert passed out after the second girl was born. Mrs. McCarter had confided in Dr. Hawkins that she was secretly praying for all girls, and her prayers were answered. Each girl was born weighing just under 3 lbs and was rushed to the neonatal intensive care unit. They would need to stay in the hospital until they were at least 6 lbs and drinking at least 4 oz of milk every 4 hours.

Mr. McCarter thanked Grant, the nurses, and all the other staff profusely once he awakened. He just kept saying, "Thank you, Jesus," and hugging everyone. Grant had never seen a new dad that excited about becoming a father, much less to three girls. Prayer had to be a big part of the McCarter's life.

Grant envisioned a future just like the McCarter's minus the triplets. He wanted to be that happy and thankful when he and his wife would have children. After the delivery, he decided to grab a cup of coffee in the hospital's cantina. Grant was still thinking about Kaleigh and getting her to go on a date with him. If he kept up the gentle pressure, she would have to fold, eventually. He started smiling again, and that was how Mr. McCarter found him.

"Doc, I can't stop thanking everyone. God really outdid himself this time and truly blessed my family. But, if it wasn't for you, I wouldn't be standing here right now. If there is anything you need, anything I can do, you just ask."

"Robert, I appreciate the offer, but I do what I do because of families like yours."

"Well, 'thank you' just doesn't seem like enough. If you fish, I have this cabin up north. Nothing fancy, but it's on the lake. You are welcomed to use it anytime. If we hadn't had to move into a bigger house to accommodate the girls, I would invite you for dinner, but Renee is still decorating. We closed on our new home last month and just put the old house on the market. Hey, you know anyone looking to buy? We have a 4-bedroom, 4 bathrooms, 4200 sq. feet house on the reservoir. Renee said it was too close to the water for little kids."

Grant was trying to process everything Robert was saying. The man didn't take a breath between sentences. But, hearing the man had an empty house, gave Grant an idea.

"Robert, let me run something by you."

65

Chapter 6

Each morning when Kaleigh woke, she prayed for healing and understanding. Over the years, her body was increasingly betraying her. The pains and aches were becoming unbearable.

She started each day by reciting her favorite bible verse, *Proverbs 4:5 Trust in the Lord with all thy heart and lean not on your own understanding.* She believed God would answer her prayers in His time. She didn't need to understand His timing, no matter how desperately she wanted answers.

Kaleigh had been feeling much better over the past few days. She promised her sisters she would make an appointment with her doctor to discuss the additional health concerns she was having. Being honest with herself, she wanted to know what was happening within her body. The whole process of testing and waiting for results was getting frustrating. Her patience was wearing thin.

If the doctors couldn't figure out what was wrong with her, she didn't know what she would do next. Suffering in silence was no longer an option; she needed answers. Kaleigh had to keep fighting and not take any half-concocted diagnosis from the doctors. There had to be real answers for her.

Her office was unusually quiet for a Friday morning when Kaleigh arrived to work. She opened her doors to find Janice and Regina huddled over Janice's computer. Neither appeared to notice her at first. Kaleigh cleared her throat to get their attention, causing Regina to jump. Nothing rattled Janice, though; she casually looked up from her monitor and smiled.

"Did I interrupt something?" Kaleigh asked.

"I didn't hear you come in," Regina stammered.

Kaleigh didn't like how she was acting. Why would she need to be so jumpy? These two were up to something.

"Where is Carl? Didn't he have an appointment with Dr. Hawkins this morning?"

"About that…Carl quit last night."

"What? What do you mean he quit? He was in the office last night when I left. He was making plans to show Dr. Hawkins a new house this week."

Janice shrugged her shoulders and said, "He sent me an email late last night stating he wasn't coming back. His only client was Dr. Hawkins, so he didn't leave anything that needed to be addressed. We don't owe him any commissions, so there is nothing left to do but officially terminate his employment contract."

Kaleigh couldn't believe the audacity of Carl to just quit in the middle of the night with an open client. Janice tried to tell her something was going on with him, but Kaleigh always wanted to give him the benefit of the doubt. He was young and often acted like other agents couldn't help him with his clients. He was a "know-it-all" like her grandmother would say.

When Carl started with the office, he was eager to learn. He had just passed his licensing exams and was enthusiastic about learning the real estate business from the bottom up. In his first year, he was the top salesperson, twice. But, in the second year, his enthusiastic demeanor was gone and replaced with arrogance.

Kaleigh started rubbing her temples and walking toward her office. She placed her coat and purse on the rack behind her desk and went to the adjoining bathroom to wash her hands. By the time she sat at her desk, Janice was handing her a cup of tea, and Regina was right behind her. They both took a seat in the chairs facing Kaleigh's desk.

"There's more, isn't there?" Kaleigh asked.

"Yes, Todd is going to be out for the next six weeks with a broken leg," Regina added to the news of the day.

"*WHAT*?" Kaleigh screamed.

"He was playing basketball and tried to dunk the ball. He came down on his right leg the wrong way. Janice was helping me to go through his workload," Regina continued.

"That means I must take on Dr. Hawkins," Kaleigh released an exasperated sigh and dropped her head into her hands.

"Kaleigh, why don't you give him a chance? He seems sincere," Janice asked, using her soft yet, stern, motherly voice.

"He has a reputation with the ladies," Kaleigh provided as an excuse not to accept his advances. She also couldn't dismiss that her sister disliked the man.

"I heard it's a bunch of baloney. My niece was at an event with him a few months ago. So many ladies approached him, and at the end of the night, he went home alone," Janice folded her arms across her chest.

"How do you know he went home alone?" Regina questioned Janice. "He could have met up with one of those women later in the evening."

Completely ignoring Regina, Janice continued, "My niece noticed how every woman who approached him walked away angry because he turned them down."

"How does your niece know about every woman that night?" Regina didn't sound convinced that Grant went home alone.

"Because she was patiently waiting for her turn and gave up when he showed no interest in not one of those women. And, he left early. One woman thought he was gay because she got nowhere with him," Janice answered.

Kaleigh took into consideration everything Janice said. Maybe she was right about Grant. Possibly he wasn't a womanizer. Kyna only said he seemed to enjoy the attention. He did seem to be sincere at the gala, and each time she took him to view a home, he wasn't pushy.

Perhaps she was being too hard on him. There was nothing wrong with taking him up on one dinner. It would also give her a chance to explain things to him; she was career-focused and not interested in a relationship.

Besides, Kaleigh couldn't dismiss what her sister had told her. He did have women that called him at the hospital. And, she had her medical issues to deal with, she didn't need the distraction. The timing just wasn't right for the two of them; she would have to keep things on a professional level.

Janice had finished reassigning Todd's clients when a request came through for a house in Raven Hills. That area of the city was historical and known for the most prestigious homes in the state. The neighborhood was a who's who for entertainers, athletes, and celebrities.

"The music producer Robert McCarter wants you to list his home. A mutual friend referred him," Janice announced.

"I'm sure I don't have a mutual friend with Robert McCarter," Kaleigh responded. She was thinking about the people she knew and the clients she has had. The only connection she could remember would come from Simon or Nick. They were the only two people who knew people in those circles.

"Well, he asked if you would be able to meet him at his house later today to do a walk-through and take pictures for the listing. I told him you could squeeze him in about 4 pm. Is that okay?" Janice asked.

"Sure, that sounds good; it would be on my way home. Call to confirm for me."

Kaleigh loved driving through the streets of Ravens Hill. Amazed by the size and architecture of the homes in this area, she marveled at the houses built in Indiana limestone and the ones that had an old castle feel to them. The large stone structures, some with architectural turrets, made Kaleigh feel like she was in Ireland.

She arrived at the address and just sat in awe of the beautiful house before her. The landscaping was meticulous, and the home appeared loved. She could see the roof was new and jotted that down in her notebook. She then leisurely walked along the pathway leading up to the front door and noticed the G4-Mostert security system, which was top of the line. That was a plus for any buyer.

The front entrance had a clear glass screen door and a beautiful solid wood door with a stained-glass window. Kaleigh rang the doorbell a few times with no answer. She noticed the heavy door, slightly ajar, and heard music playing. Instead of ringing the bell again, she pushed the door further open and entered.

"Hello! Mr. McCarter? Is anyone here?" she announced.

Suddenly, a man dressed in a formal tuxedo appeared from seemingly out of nowhere. Kaleigh jumped at his sudden appearance.

"Hello, Ms. Hammond. My name is Henson," he said with a slight bow. "Please allow me to escort you to the back of the house," He held out his arm to her, and she accepted.

Why hadn't he answered the door when she first arrived? Henson had a British accent and seemed a little overdressed to be answering doors. She guessed he was the housekeeper or butler. *Of course, Mr. McCarter would have a butler.* Her heart began to calm as she walked with Henson, along the way admiring the furnishings and decor.

They continued through a set of beautiful stained-glass double doors that matched the front entrance and led to a patio area. Kaleigh dropped her jaw when she saw Grant standing by a table beautifully decorated and set for two. She thought Grant looked handsome in his black suit and dark blue tie. He had sex-appeal oozing from him and causing Kaleigh to become a little weak in the knees.

His gaze was staring right into her soul. She wasn't able to speak; instead, she looked away and noticed the table, floral arrangements, the lights, and the musicians seated on the far side of the patio.

Grant stalked toward her carrying two glasses of wine. She finally found her voice and asked, "What are you doing here?"

"I referred you to Robert and told him you were the best realtor in the state. I also asked him for a favor since I just successfully delivered his daughters," he handed her the second glass. "I hope you like sweet wines; I have a fondness for this Riesling. I purchase it from a family-owned winery in Napa Valley. I would love to take you there one day."

Kaleigh hadn't heard anything Grant said. She was trying to understand how she seemed to be suddenly attracted to him. In previous interactions, he was annoying, and now he was alluring. While sitting in her office, she had decided to give Mr. Grant a chance to talk. Nothing more, just talk. Now, she wasn't sure if she would be able to hold a conversation with him. His intense looks and deep voice was causing her to shiver.

She accepted the glass and drained the contents in one gulp. She didn't mean to do that, but she needed something to quench the blazing fire inside of her.

"Maybe I should get you some water or iced tea first. I'm not sure you tasted the wine," Grant laughed, taking the glass from her hand.

Kaleigh was finding it difficult to think straight and vaguely remembered Grant gently taking her hand and leading her to the romantic scene he had set-up. The table décor included a full bouquet of red, pink, and white roses and several red and white candles on top of a white tablecloth.

"I had the chef prepare several dishes. I didn't know what you would like, or if you had any allergies," Grant said to her while he pulled her chair back, allowing her to sit.

"Grant, this is beautiful. But I'm still confused. Why did you do all of this?" she asked.

"Kaleigh, I wanted to take you out, get to know you, but you kept saying no. I had to do something drastic to get your attention. So, I decided to bring dinner to you instead." Grant rubbed his hands over his head and took a deep breath. "Honestly, I just want to get to know you better."

Still standing, Kaleigh tried to keep the edge from her voice. "Dr. Hawkins, what if I don't want to...." She stopped mid-sentence when she smelled the most divine scent filter beneath her nose. "What am I smelling?"

Grant smiled, "That is dinner; please, have a seat." He motioned to the chair he was holding out for her. Kaleigh still had not moved. She was skeptical of Grant's intentions. He kept saying he wanted to get to know her, but in her limited experience, that meant he wanted something more, and she just wasn't in a place to give him more.

The loud wailing of her stomach overturned her objection to his romantic dinner in protest. "Since you went through a lot of trouble, I will indulge you this one time," she took the seat he offered and watched as he nodded to someone in the house and then sat in the chair opposite of her.

A server, dressed in a tuxedo, placed salads in front of them, then disappeared into the house. Kaleigh reached for her fork but noticed that Grant had his hands extended to her. She had forgotten entirely to bless her food. She sheepishly smiled and placed her hands into his larger ones. Kaleigh immediately noticed how soft they were and how he gently closed his hands over hers and began praying.

The private chef had prepared a beef, a chicken, and a fish dinner. Grant didn't know what she would prefer, so he wanted to give her options. Kaleigh appreciated the thought and selected the baked rosemary chicken with a side of mixed vegetables and a creamy sweet potato souffle. Along with their meal, she also enjoyed the conversation she shared with Grant. He wasn't nearly as arrogant as Kyna first made him out to be.

She learned that he decided on the medical field after a bet with his mother. She used parental reverse psychology to get Grant to realize his full potential. His mother bet him $2,000 that he couldn't graduate from high school in the top 5% of his class. When he graduated as the valedictorian, she doubled the wager for college. She then tripled the bet, saying he wouldn't get accepted into medical school.

By the time he graduated from Meharry Medical School, Grant had found out that the money she was betting with was his all along. His grandfather had left each of his siblings a trust fund to be distributed on their 25th birthday. His mother got a good laugh when he found out.

Kaleigh also learned that obstetrics and gynecology was not his first choice. Grant had wanted to be a pediatrician, but after finding out about his mother's history of complications with pregnancies, he decided to change focus. Grant wanted to help women get pregnant and also spend time researching reproduction therapies.

Overall, Kaleigh was impressed with Grant as a man and a doctor. She didn't want to admit it, but his kindness and humble attitude deepened her initial physical attraction to him. When dessert arrived, Kaleigh had to decline. Her stomach was full from the scrumptious meal that his chef had prepared and couldn't possibly eat another bite.

"Grant, thank you for dinner. It was delicious and much appreciated. I need to be leaving now."

****

Grant wasn't ready for her to leave. The evening had been perfect thus far. She hadn't outwardly resisted him, but he could see in her eyes that she wanted to run away. He knew she could feel the attraction brewing between them, and he would bet his medical license that scared her.

He didn't want to be pushy; Grant was excited that she stayed this long and even seemed to relax during their meal.

"You can't leave," Grant said.

"Grant, it was nice talking with you, but I have…" she tried to explain.

"No, I mean, you still need to take the pictures of the rooms. And I haven't given you a tour yet." Grant knew she was trying to put distance between them. Bringing up business was a great way to keep her near for a little while longer.

"You mean to tell me, Robert McCarter really wants me to list his home? This wasn't just a ploy by you to have dinner with me?"

Grant laughed. "He really wants you to list his home." Rising from his chair, he reached for Kaleigh's hand. "We can begin upstairs and work our way down to the basement."

Grant was, again, impressed with Kaleigh. He expected her to use her cell phone to take pictures; instead, she pulled out a professional digital camera. In each room, she took photos from different angles to get the best views of the room. She then created some short video clips of areas like the master bedroom closets, the laundry room, the hallways leading to each room, and the basement area.

She was finishing up the pictures of the office in the basement when she saw an elegantly wrapped gift on a bookshelf with her name on a gift tag. Kaleigh was hesitant to touch the gift, so Grant walked over to the bookshelf and held it out for her.

"I hope you like it."

Grant held his breath as she slowly and meticulously removed the wrapping paper. Her eyes seemed to double in size as she recognized the book she was holding in her hands.

"This is a collection of poems by Edgar Allen Poe. Not just any collection, this is the first edition released by the Evening Mirror in 1846. This is amazing, but how did you know?"

"A little birdie told me," he smiled.

"Yeah, I bet there were three little birdies," she referred to her sisters.

"Honestly, only one of your sisters talks to me. She said something after I questioned why everyone called you Poe."

Grant watched her continue to rub her fingers over the cover. She had yet to open the book or look at the pages. While she marveled at the cover, he watched her intently.

"Thank you. This is the best present I've ever received. My sisters and my parents never understood me growing up. When I started reading Poe and all of his mysteries, I found something that set me apart from my sisters. Then one day, my grandmother called me every K name she could think of before finally settling on saying, "You, I'm talking to you." It's not that she was senile or anything, it was just too many K names in my house. So, I thought I would help everyone out and demanded everyone call me Poe." Kaleigh let a tear escape and roll down her face.

"Kaleigh, are you okay?" He used his thumb to wipe away the tear.

"I'm sorry, Grant. My head has been hurting all day, and the pain just intensified. And every time I take a breath, my chest tightens and starts to hurt. I don't know what is going on with me."

"Here, take a seat. Tell me, what are your symptoms?"

Poe took a seat in an overstuffed chair, and Grant kneeled down in front of her. She began to explain all of her ailments over the past few months and years. She was preparing herself to be lectured to as Kyna would occasionally do. Instead, Grant massaged her hands, paying particular attention to her pressure points.

"Kaleigh, I don't want to see you in any pain. It sounds like you are taking care of yourself and seeing a doctor when you need to.

I'm not going trying to diagnose you because I am not your doctor. I just want to be your friend and be here for you."

Grant was unbelievable. He was behaving the exact opposite of what she had been told about him. Maybe Janice was right about him after all; maybe he was a nice guy and not the arrogant, self-centered doctor she thought him to be. The soothing of her hand massage reduced the pain in her head, but not in her chest. Kaleigh instinctively took a deep breath and doubled over in pain.

Grant scooped her into his arms and started for his car.

"I'm taking you to the hospital. Something is not right," he said before she could refuse.

Chapter 7

It had been two weeks since the episode Poe had at the McCarter house with Grant. She would be forever grateful to him for taking her to the hospital. He even saw that her car was taken to her home, and he had called her sisters and parents to let them know what had happened.

Poe didn't want to admit it, but Grant was behaving almost like a boyfriend. She shook her head, not wanting to believe that he could actually be the man that Janice said he was. He stayed with her at the hospital until her family arrived. She could tell he was feeling tossed aside, especially once her father arrived and completely dismissed him. At least Karmyn and Kyna talked to him while she was being poked and prodded.

At the hospital, Poe had to take several tests, EKG's, ECG's, bloodwork, the whole gamut. After a full day of testing, the ER doctor finally diagnosed her with pleurisy. Pleurisy was an inflammation of the tissue that lined the lungs and chest cavity, causing pain that worsens when breathing,

But that didn't explain the migraines, the fainting, or the other symptoms she had. The doctor had told her the best recourse for pleurisy was to take steroids and rest, but the last time she took a steroid treatment, she had trouble sleeping and gained a lot of weight. Poe refused the steroids and opted for plenty of rest and anti-inflammatory drugs instead.

After resting for the past two weeks, she needed to get out of the house. She had not been to church in a few weeks and was feeling a little anxious about going to the seminar that Grant and Kyna were presenting to the congregation on health risks. Poe knew she would get lots of questions about her disappearance and was mentally preparing to face everyone. Only the choir director was aware of her health issues, and he didn't know them all.

Poe entered the fellowship hall of her church from the side door and walked to the back of the room, where Karleigh sat alone playing on her cell phone.

"Why are you sitting in the back of the room?" Poe asked.

"Because I know most of the information they are presenting. Kyna was nervous and practiced her material on me all week."

"Oh, okay." Poe took a seat next to her sister, trying not to make any noise. There appeared to be a full house; approximately 60-75 women were in attendance.

"How are you feeling? Mama said you haven't been back to work yet." Karleigh asked, never looking up from her phone.

"No, I'm going back next week. Janice has been holding down the fort for me."

"I just love Janice; she is the best."

Poe thought the very same thing. Aside from family, Janice was the very best friend you could have. She bordered on motherly and sisterly and knew when to step into each role.

For the next hour, Poe and Karleigh sat in the back of the room and listened to their baby sister present on obesity in the community and the importance of healthy eating and healthy lifestyles. Afterward, Grant spoke on other health issues women were plagued with like heart disease and the different types of female cancers: cervical, ovarian, and breast.

Together, Grant and Kyna conducted blood pressure checks and blood sugar testing on everyone in attendance. Two women were sent immediately to the emergency room due to their test results. Grant was sure one was having a heart attack as she sat there.

After the educational session, Kyna scheduled a woman to come in to give a Zumba class and a low-impact line dancing class. There was also a healthy cooking session and a few non-profit health organizations sharing information. The afternoon turned out to be better than anyone expected, with over 150 women attending in total. The first lady of the church thanked Grant profusely for possibly saving the lives of many women in the room, not just the two he sent to the hospital.

Poe wore a cheesy smile that caught the interest of Karleigh.

"Why are you looking like that?"

"Like what?" she replied, still smirking.

"Like you are a proud mama."

"Because I am so proud of Kyna. She really blossomed into a brilliant woman and nurse," Poe wiped a tear that slowly descended from her eye.

"Poe, stop with the games. You have been staring at Dr. Hawkins. You didn't hear a word, Kyna said. You are so full of it," Karleigh laughed.

Poe didn't even try to hide the truth from her sister. She was just as proud of Grant as she was of Kyna. The two of them worked together well as a team. She could see how they would work well together in the hospital.

Instead of trading words with her sister, she stood and walked over to the doctor. He was standing in a circle of women who were throwing questions at him left and right.

"Ladies, I specialize in obstetrics. If you want better answers to those questions, please schedule with your primary care physician."

Poe overheard one lady say, "My primary care doctor doesn't look like him." She laughed because she could agree. Her doctor was an older Asian man.

"Ladies, please excuse, I must speak with Ms. Hammond before she leaves."

One lady looked rebuffed as he walked past her, the others nodded and walked away in different directions.

"Dr. Hawkins, you and Nurse Kyna work well together," Kaleigh complimented him.

"Thank you, Poe. Is it okay to call you Poe? I realized that only your family calls you that."

She smiled and said, "A few friends call me Poe, also. I guess I will consider you a friend, for now." She tucked a stray strand of hair behind her ear, trying to appear demure. She had no idea why, suddenly, she was feeling nervous around the doctor.

*****

Grant was excited to see Kaleigh when she entered the room. He didn't care that she may have been there to support her sister. The only thing that mattered was she was there. Occasionally, he would glance toward the back of the room, where she sat with her sister and made eye contact with her a few times.

When he left her in the hospital a few weeks ago, he felt like he was leaving a friend behind in her time of need. Her sisters had arrived, then her parents and he felt pushed out of the way. At least Karmyn thanked him for being there for her. Only Kyna and Karmyn knew about his interest in Poe. Karleigh was wrapped in her wedding details; he didn't think she had noticed.

Nevertheless, she was here standing in front of him, and he was just as happy to see her feeling a lot better.

Grant was nervous and wasn't sure what to say or where to start. He wanted to ask her about her diagnosis or about looking at another house. But, neither topic seemed appropriate at the moment.

Feeling more relaxed, he asked, "Would you like to have a cup of coffee with me? There is a small bookstore not far from here with amazing white chocolate mocha."

He hadn't realized he was holding his breath, awaiting a response until she agreed to meet with him. Grant tried to keep his excitement level down. This was the second time she surprised him by saying yes.

"Let me finish up some things here, pack up my equipment, and meet you there."

"Sure, I'll tell my sisters' goodbye."

Grant couldn't believe that his fortune with Kaleigh was turning around. She was being agreeable to having coffee with him. In the past, she would have declined the offer. He didn't care why she was having a change of heart; he was going to use it to his advantage.

In less than 10 minutes, he was packed up and in his car. The bookstore was only five blocks away, and as luck would have it, there was a parking space right next to Kaleigh's vehicle.

Call it fate, but maybe he was starting to wear down her resistance. Ever since the dinner at the house, she was much more pleasant. He liked this turn of events that had her smiling at him. Being patient was working out for him.

Grant spotted Poe in line, getting a cup of coffee. Before she could pull out her wallet, he swooped in with his credit card. "I'll take care of that for you."

He also ordered a latte for himself, and they found a cozy spot near the back of the bookstore. They were surrounded by walls of used books in various genres.

"You know, when I was a kid, I would spend hours in the library, trying to read anything and everything. I loved reading," she reminisced.

"Loved, as in past tense?" he asked.

After taking a sip, she responded, "I just don't have the time to read anymore. I keep pretty busy with my office. I'm small potatoes compared to the Remax's of the world."

"You seem to be doing pretty well for yourself. The deal with my brother seems to be going well."

"Do you keep up with your brother's business?" she asked.

The family business was a topic he never discussed with the women in his life. Often, they were only interested in how much money the company made. Doing a little research, you could find out that Grant was a successful doctor, sought after around the world. But the extent of his wealth was a well-guarded secret. He didn't believe his siblings knew just how wealthy he was.

His college roommate was a financial genius, and he trusted everything Henry said to do. Those earlier investments proved to be very fruitful and netted him over five million dollars before he graduated from medical school. The other aspect of his wealth that many didn't know was he was a silent partner with Morgan. When his brother started his company, Grant was the first onboard. Melissa was still in high school, and John was John, the ultimate skirt chaser in college.

Their father gave Morgan a $100,000 loan to be paid back in 10 years, but Grant pitched in a silent million dollars. Morgan was overwhelmed by the gift and offered a partnership instead.

Grant believed in his brother, just as he believed in Kaleigh. She had the same type of determination that he saw in his brother and himself.

"My brother is the best at what he does. I try to stay out of family business as much as possible. Besides, his business and mine don't exactly go together."

That got a laugh out of her, and for the first time since meeting Kaleigh, she appeared relaxed. Her smile lit up the room, and her laughter was infectious. Before long, he was laughing along with her.

They talked about their families and the differences in their childhoods. They both had three siblings and a host of shenanigans that went on. Grant could see Karmyn as the troublemaker. He didn't have to convince Kaleigh that John was a playboy in the making. He told her the story about John sneaking out of the house to go to the mall when they were 14-years-old; all because John wanted to meet some girls, and Grant didn't want him to get into any serious trouble.

The bookstore was closing, and the manager informed them they could stay a while longer while he cleaned up. They declined his offer and walked outside, allowing the manager to lock the doors behind them.

"Have we really been here for six hours?" Kaleigh asked.

"It doesn't feel like it." They were standing between their two cars. An awkward silence ensued for several seconds.

They both tried to speak at once.

"I apologize. Ladies first," Grant offered.

"I enjoyed my time with you. Today was the first day in quite a while that I felt normal. Thank you. I needed a friend to talk to that wasn't a relative."

"Anytime. You know, I can't get with calling you, Poe. Do you mind if I keep calling you Kaleigh? I promise never to confuse you with your sisters."

They both laughed. He watched how she shyly tucked her head and her nervous action of moving a non-existent strand of hair behind her ear.

"I like it when you call me Kaleigh. Mostly only clients and bill collectors call me that."

They laughed again, neither seeming to want to get in their cars and drive away.

"When do you go back to work? I think I want to make an offer on one of the houses," Grant asked, putting his hands in his pockets and shifting from one foot to the other.

"I will be in the office on Monday. Stop by anytime."

Before Grant could fully understand what he was doing, he gently used his index finger to raise her chin. He stared into her eyes for several seconds before leaning in for a brief kiss to the forehead.

"Good night, Kaleigh. See you on Monday."

Grant opened the door to her car and made sure she was buckled in before closing the door. He then slid into his vehicle and waited for her to pull away first.

The day was almost perfect until he looked at his cell phone, another call and five text messages. He had been trying to ignore her, but she wouldn't go away.

Chapter 8

The first house Grant selected already had an offer, and he lost out on that deal. Kaleigh was sure Grant didn't mind; it would give him cause to spend more time with her. Over the past few weeks, they had met for coffee a few times and once for dinner. They truly enjoyed one another's company.

They looked at a few more houses closer to the downtown area, but Grant was indecisive. If she didn't know better, she would think he wasn't interested in a house at all.

The deal for the Hawkins group was successful, and Kaleigh would be closing that deal in the next few days with a symbolic groundbreaking scheduled for a few weeks later. The Hawkins Group decided on the historic building near the medical district. There would be no demolition, so the ceremony was simply for good public relations and the media.

The mayor, and possibly even the governor, were expected to attend. So far, Melissa Hawkins was doing a great job of creating excitement around the event. That effort also extended to K. Hammond Realty. Kaleigh was being swamped with appointments from key investors and everyday people looking for a home. She was also able to hire two additional agents to help with the load. Regina and Todd were promoted to handle higher-end clients.

Kaleigh was waiting for Janice to bring her some closing documents when she started feeling fatigued and sluggish. She felt like she had run a mile at full speed and couldn't seem to catch her breath. When Janice entered her office, she could barely speak.

"Kaleigh, sit down. Let me call 911."

"No! I don't need 911. It will pass, I promise," she spoke between breaths. Her movements seemed to happen in slow-motion, and her joints were feeling achy. Kaleigh initially thought it was the pleurisy returning, but she wasn't getting that same pain when she inhaled. She tried to lift her head, and everything in her body seemed heavy.

"Janice, can you get me a cup of the peach green tea. I will be alright," Kaleigh reassured her.

Janice stood in place and watched her for a few minutes before going off to get her the tea. Kaleigh was getting tired of not knowing what was going on with her body. She had been dealing with the migraines and pleurisy for a while, but this feeling was new. She had never been out of breath without doing anything physical. The body aches and fatigue were also new since her last visit to the doctor.

With her tea, Kaleigh quickly took two anti-inflammatory pills and kicked her feet up on the sofa in her office. She was trying to rest and let the medicine take effect when Karmyn burst through the door.

"Are you alright?"

"Oh my God, did Janice call you?" Kaleigh said slowly.

"No, I was on my way here to take you to lunch, and she told me you were having an episode." Karmyn sat on the sofa next to her sister.

"Well, no need to worry; it was just that, an episode. And it has passed," Kaleigh lied to her sister. She didn't want her trying to play doctor and convincing her she needed yet another ER visit.

"Kaleigh, you don't look well, and your ankles look swollen." She moved some pillows under her feet to help elevate them. When grabbing her feet, Karmyn stopped and looked more closely at Kaleigh's legs. She felt around on her knees then looked scared.

"Sister, what's wrong?"

"Your knees are swollen, too. Did you know that?"

Kaleigh looked down at her legs and noticed that her knees were slightly puffy. "No, I didn't realize it," Kaleigh said. She was trying to hold back the tears. The pain and now the swelling were too much for her to deal with. Her health issues were too much for someone of her age. She was still in her twenties, and her body felt like she was in her eighties. Kaleigh slightly prayed that God would intervene for her and help her doctors find out what has been causing her years of pain.

"Sister, I'm not a doctor, and I am not Kyna, but there is something wrong, and now is not the time to shut your sisters out. This isn't right. Either I take you to the hospital, or I call 911. I will let you make a choice." Karmyn held her phone in the air, letting Kaleigh know she was not bluffing.

Kaleigh didn't have to think long when she took a deep breath, and the pain in her chest tightened. She acquiesced and allowed Janice and her sister to help her stand.

They walked her slowly to Karmyn's car; Kaleigh was experiencing pain in every joint as she took a step. Getting into the car was difficult and took a few additional minutes to adjust. On the way to the emergency room, Kaleigh's head started to pound harder. They had to turn the music off, even though it was playing very low. Karmyn called Karleigh en route to the hospital. She couldn't reach Kyna, so she left a message instead, hoping her sister was in the hospital.

Karleigh met them at the door to the emergency room. The hospital staff was able to get Kaleigh inside and admitted quickly.

After five hours of testing, an emergency room doctor entered the room, along with Kyna.

"Ms. Hammond, I have been reviewing your test results from all of your visits within the past year. Has anyone ever told you, you are anemic?" The ER doctor was younger than the last few doctors Kaleigh had seen. The glasses on his face seemed to slide down to the edge of his nose as he was reading her charts.

"No, not that I can remember," Kaleigh responded. That's just more information that didn't add up.

"Well, I want to do one more test. I want to do a biopsy of your kidney."

"A biopsy!" the three sisters said aloud.

"I want to wait for the results, but it's to rule out some other things. We can do the biopsy in the next hour, and then I want to keep you overnight. Is that okay with everyone?" The doctor asked.

"Doctor, she will do whatever you want her to do," Kyna answered for her sister.

"Okay, I will let my team know. Don't worry, Ms. Hammond, I will get to the bottom of this."

The doctor left the room, and all eyes were on Kaleigh. She was aware that her sisters wanted answers. She had never told them how many visits she made to the emergency room in the past two years or the many doctor's appointments she had.

"Lucy, you got some 'splaining to do," Karleigh imitated Ricky Ricardo.

"Promise me you won't tell Mommy and Daddy until we know what is truly going on." She made each sister promise before she pulled her cell phone from her purse.

Poe kept meticulous records of her health and kept track of her symptoms and dates she visited the doctor or hospital on her phone. She told her sisters about all the tests she has had, including the many blood tests, chest X-rays, echocardiograms, and the many different medications that have been prescribed to her.

By the time she was finished telling her sisters everything, the nurses were coming to her room to take her back for the biopsy. She returned within a few hours, and her sisters were in the very same places they had been when she left.

Poe awakened the next morning with Karmyn and Karleigh still in her room. Kyna left to check on something in her department and would return later. Poe noticed their mood had changed and seemed a bit somber.

"Hey sisters, I'll be okay," Poe whispered, trying to stay positive.

"Will you?" Karmyn asked with a note of sarcasm and a whole lot of attitude.

Poe was confused by Karmyn's attitude and wanted to question her about it, but a nurse entered her room to check on her vitals and medication. While the nurse fiddled around, Poe kept her focus on Karmyn. Poe was the one sick and in the hospital every other week, so she didn't understand her sister's attitude.

Once the nurse left the room, Poe asked, "What's your problem, Karmyn?"

"Have you told Grant about all of your health issues?" Karmyn folded her arms across her chest.

"It's not his concern. Besides, we are just friends."

"Friends or not, it's not fair to Grant to get involved with you if you have a serious health condition."

"Dang sister, that's cold," Karleigh responded.

"But it's true. Wouldn't you want to know if Simon was dying of some illness?" Karmyn turned to Karleigh.

"I'm not dying," Poe interjected. This was the very reason she had not told her family about all of her health issues. They tended to go overboard. The doctors still didn't know what was going on in her body, and her sister had already put her on her deathbed. "The doctors don't know what is wrong with me. I have chronic, debilitating migraines that could be the cause of my passing out. I also have pleurisy, which causes chest pains. You don't know what it's like not to know what is going on in your body. So, stop talking to me," Poe yelled at Karmyn.

"Well, do what you want to. I've said my peace," Karmyn pouted, folding her arms across her chest like she used to do when they were kids.

The silence in the room was louder than the machines periodically sounding off. Poe's sisters may be angry with one another, but it never interfered with their sisterhood. They would never leave each alone in their time of need. Instead of talking or arguing any further, they sat in comfortable silence. The mood in the room shifted around lunchtime.

Instead of the food service worker bringing her lunch, the cart was rolled in by Dr. Hawkins himself.

"Room service," he announced.

"Well, look who we have here…Dr. Hawkins. It's good to see you here," Karmyn said, then gave Poe a death stare.

"Grant, how did you know I was here?" Poe asked.

"Kyna told me. I hope it's alright," he said and looked around at the saddened faces of her sisters. "Had I known Karmyn and Karleigh were here, I would have brought more food; as it is, I'm not sure if you can have this." He removed the plastic dome to reveal a white paper bag.

"Is that what I think it is?" Poe struggled to sit upright.

"Sure is. Chicken shawarma from Persia's with a side of hummus."

"I could kiss you," she replied, temporarily forgetting her sisters were in the room.

"Interesting. Well, Sister, I think we should go and find our own lunch," Karleigh suggested, standing and nodding to Karmyn.

"I agree. We'll be back, Poe." Karmyn's eyes widened, giving her a look that was meant to nudge her into telling Grant about her health issues.

Poe considered telling him everything she had shared with her sisters but was afraid of his reaction. Allowing Grant to continue pursuing her without having the facts wasn't fair to him. She hated it when her sisters were right, especially when it was Karmyn.

"Grant, I need to tell….."

"Whatever it is, can you tell me later? I heard from a reliable source that you are going home soon, and I have something special planned." Grant shoved one end of his shawarma in his mouth, smiling, easing the tension she felt. Poe was grateful for Grant and his friendship. She was also finding it difficult to resist his persistent charm. He was very easy to talk to and wasn't pushy. She never felt like she was forcibly persuaded into anything.

"Something special, like what?" she asked while dipping her carrots into the hummus.

"It is a surprise." He smiled, wrapped the remainder of his sandwich in the bag, and stood to leave.

"Where are you going?" Kaleigh was disappointed he wasn't going to stay a little while longer.

"I have a few things to take care of before I can leave for the day. Then, I am coming back to get you and take you away from this place." He scrunched his face and motioned around like the hospital room was a horrible place.

Poe couldn't help but laugh at his silliness. "I will be here waiting."

*****

Grant couldn't believe the past few weeks with Kaleigh had been nothing but bliss. Sure, they were just on a friend level, and she was still hesitant to move their relationship any further, but that's a long way from where he started.

Over the weeks, they had continued to meet at the bookstore once a week for coffee and conversation. A poetry slam event was taking place one week, and they discovered they both enjoyed listening to the spoken word, but neither dared to stand on the stage and allow themselves to be open and vulnerable in front of a crowd.

The evenings they would spend together ended with Grant seeing that Kaleigh made it home safely, then a phone call to her when he made it back to his condo. The nights when they didn't go out, Grant made sure to call Kaleigh before she went to bed. Every nightly conversation, they would pray with each other before saying good night. Their calls were the best part of his day. He learned something new every time he talked with her.

Grant planned for the two of them to go to the lake and have a picnic after she was released from the hospital. He enjoyed watching the sunset and wanted to share that with her. He never thought in a million years he would be planning cute little dates with a woman. Grant typically dated women who preferred fancy dinners in expensive restaurants and fine wine to go along with their insanely priced meals, but not Kaleigh. She wasn't in the least impressed with expensive restaurants or material things. She told him as much during one of their many conversations at the bookstore.

He remembered her saying she was more impressed by the thought and effort put into planning a date than the amount of money someone spent. The shock on his face caused her to laugh…Not just smile, but really relax and laugh at him. He knew of no other woman like her, except maybe his sister and his mother.

Grant was floating on cloud nine, whistling down the hallway when he ran into Kyna and the medical director of the hospital.

"Dr. Hawkins, Nurse Kyna and I were just looking for you," the medical director announced.

"Nothing bad, I hope," he joked.

"On the contrary. I was hoping you would be able to attend a hospital fundraiser today in my place. It seems my wife is not feeling well, and I will be heading home. Nurse Kyna is on the fundraising committee, and she offered to walk you through the event."

Kyna gave them both the cheesiest and fakest smiles. Grant wasn't sure what the event was or what he would be required to do, but turning down the director was a big no if you wanted to keep your career. He was a well-respected doctor and held the power to destroy you in one hand. If he asked you to do something, you did it.

"Why, of course. I would be honored."

"Great! Well, you two get along, the carnival will be starting soon." The director continued down the hall, leaving Grant staring at Kyna as she increased her smile.

"Carnival!" he quietly exclaimed for Kyna's ears only. "You set me up."

"Whatever do you mean, Dr. Hawkins?" She laughed and began walking toward the hospital courtyard. "Follow me. The dunk tank awaits you."

"Dunk tank? How long will this take? I had plans for later."

"The director volunteered for the dunk booth, and then he was to be the master of ceremonies for the awards ceremony. I would say we should be all done by 5 or 6 pm."

That meant he would not be able to take Kaleigh to the lake. He would have to cancel on her, and he hoped she would understand. Pulling his phone from his pocket, he noticed a few missed calls and text messages from someone he was trying to forget. Deleting those messages, he sent Kaleigh a quick text message detailing the situation her sister put him in while he walked with Kyna to the carnival.

Grant wasn't sure how he missed the massive event set-up in the hospital's courtyard and parking lot. There was a ferris wheel, several carnival games, and a few food trucks. Half the hospital seemed to be outside enjoying themselves.

Grant was sitting in the dunk tank, allowing nurses, patients, children, and their parents to throw balls in an attempt to drop him into the water. So far, only three nurses and one teenager were able to hit the target. The nurses seemed to be out to get him, especially the blonde from the Intensive Care Unit. She had asked him on several dates, and he declined each of them.

The teenager dropped him on the first throw and then told Grant he was a baseball pitcher for his high school. Grant was beginning to enjoy trash-talking the participants who couldn't hit the target. The next person in line was the woman from his past that he had been ignoring for several weeks.

She tossed the ball in the air like she would really throw it. But, Grant knew this woman very well, and she wouldn't dare ruin her perfect manicure to throw a ball. She used her left hand to run her fingers through her long tresses and then handed the ball to the teenager.

"$100 if you sink him on the first try," she offered.

"No problem, lady. That $100 is as good as mine," the teenager accepted.

With no effort, the teenager dropped Grant into the water with a loud splash.   Other onlookers were laughing and enjoying themselves, but the fun stopped when Grant realized he was going to have to deal with Hannah before he wanted to.

Grant reached for the towel to wipe the water from his face and noticed it was missing. He opened his eyes to find Hannah, holding the towel standing next to the tank.

"Well, Grant, since you wouldn't answer my calls or my text messages, it seems I had to come down here to find you." She was holding the towel hostage, toying with him, by letting him try to reach for it, then pulling it away. Grant was finally able to snatch it from her hands and dry himself off.

"What are you doing here, Hannah?" he asked angrily.

"Really, Grant, doesn't this hospital have people for this type of thing?" She waved her hand around toward the rest of the carnival.

"You shouldn't be here."

"Why? Do you have another fiancée?" She raised her voice when asking the question.

"You aren't my fiancée, either." He forcefully grabbed her hand and pulled her away from onlookers. Grant was trying to make sure none of the nurses or Kyna saw him. Instead, they ran right into Kyna, carrying a large bag of popcorn.

"Great, Dr. Hawkins, can you grab the other two bags from the cafeteria?"

Immediately he felt sick to his stomach. He was sure Hannah was about to put on a show. Drama was her middle name, and she never passed up an opportunity to put down someone she felt was beneath her.

"Don't you know who this is? Dr. Hawkins is a world-renowned physician. He doesn't do menial tasks. Can't you do it?" the venom lacing her words.

The look in Kyna's eyes was telling him he needed to get Hannah out of there quickly. He knew how Kyna could be when angered. Instead of addressing Hannah, Kyna turned to Grant. "Dr. Hawkins, we need the two bags of popcorn from the cafeteria. I sincerely hope you take care of it."

Grant was thankful that Kyna hadn't said anything else, but he was sure he was going to need to explain himself very soon. The Hammond sisters were very tight-knit, and this dramatic scene was going to get back to Kaleigh.

"What are you a nurse or something?" Hannah asked, not letting the issue rest. She eyed Kyna up and down with a distasteful look. "Listen, my fiancé has staff that does these things for him," Hannah spouted off again.

Kyna cut her off. "Fiancée? Really! Well, Fiancée, Dr. Hawkins, is a representative of this hospital and, as a representative, appointed by our medical director, who happens to be his boss, he will continue to work at this event. And, seeing as I am in charge of this event, he works for me." Turning her attention back to Grant, she said, "Make sure you are ready for the pie-eating contest when you return." Kyna emphasized the word "when" before she turned to walk away.

"They need to train these nurses. She was rude," Hannah scoffed after Kyna was out of earshot.

"Yeah, well, she is also on my service, and I have to work with her," he continued to pull Hannah through the doors and outside to the side of the building.

"Listen, Hannah, you cannot be here, and you need to leave. Now!"

"I'm not going anywhere until we talk, and you give me a chance to explain."

That made Grant angry. "Explain? There is nothing to explain. I caught you red-handed. Do you deny marrying that man while wearing my ring?" he questioned her.

Hannah rolled her eyes upward before checking out her manicure. "It's not what you think. I returned your ring, didn't I?"

"After you married him, and you returned it by courier. You didn't even have the decency to tell me to my face. I had to find out online. You humiliated me."

"Oh, Grant, don't be so dramatic. I'm no longer with Ian. He stayed in Italy, and I'm back in the states."

"So, you think I'm just supposed to kiss and make-up? Forget it, Hannah. Leave now before you get your feelings hurt."

"The only person getting their feelings hurt will be you. I'll be back." She stormed off in a huff, away from the carnival. Grant thanked God she didn't return to the carnival or go anywhere near Kyna.

Grant grabbed the bags of popcorn from the cafeteria and rushed back to the carnival. He was mentally preparing to face Kyna and explain. Instead of Kyna being angry, she excitedly continued with the activities and never let on what she was thinking. That scared Grant more than a confrontation with her.

Once the carnival was over, and Grant was able to get Kyna alone, he tried to explain who Hannah was. She pretended to listen. He could tell she didn't believe anything he was saying.

"Kyna, you, believe me, right?" Grant begged.

"Sure, but I still have to tell my sister."

"At least give me a chance to tell her myself."

"Whatever, but I'm going to tell her as soon as I see her. I will not hold this back from her. So, you better get to her before I do," Kyna turned and walked away.

Chapter 9

Fishing was one of Grant's most peaceful activities, and he had promised his brothers that they would go to the lake the next time Morgan was in town. Morgan had returned for the groundbreaking ceremony for his new hotel. Kaleigh convinced the Hawkins Group that the historic building was a great investment opportunity, and after careful and thorough research and consideration, they agreed.

Morgan was no slacker in business and knew a good deal when he saw one. The paperwork had been finalized a few weeks ago, and now the brothers were relaxing before the real work of renovations began.

"Who thought 7 am was a good time to go fishing?" John asked as he cast his line into the water.

"It's calm and less movement in the water. The fish tend to be less anxious," Morgan offered as the reason for getting started early.

"Whatever," John dismissed his brother. "What is Melissa doing today? Why didn't you make her come with us?"

"Because this is brother bonding time," Grant responded.

"Who thought *that* was a good idea?" John asked, clearly annoyed.

"Of course, it was Morgan. I just promised to go fishing, nothing about waking up before the birds," Grant laughed.

"And why do we listen to him?" John reeled in his line to cast it again.

"Because he is the oldest."

"You two knuckleheads want to keep it down over there?" Morgan chuckled as he was preparing the bait for his hook. "Besides, you act like we get to see each other all the time. I miss you two. With John overseeing the project, you two will get to see each other more. Melissa will be heading to New York next month; I'm going to be all alone."

"You like your life of solitude. Imagine having all of us underfoot all the time. It would drive you crazy," John said.

Grant was thinking the same thing about his brother. He definitely enjoyed his solitude, even when growing up, Morgan would prefer working alone.

"Well, John, how have you been spending your time?" Morgan asked.

"With the ladies, of course. This city has some beautiful women. I didn't even have to go to the strip club to find them. Although there are some nice strip clubs here, too."

"Jesus, you could do anything with your money, but decide to throw it away on strippers," Grant replied, shaking his head in disgust.

John faked innocent. "What? I'm helping to stimulate the economy."

"Grant, let him do his thing. It's his money," Morgan said.

"Thank you, big brother. Besides, I haven't been wasting too much money as of late. I found a new hobby."

"Really!?" both brothers turned in his direction.

"Don't seem so shocked. I met a woman, and she is a yoga instructor and massage therapist. She is really into naturopathic health. It's actually quite fascinating."

Grant couldn't believe his baby brother was interested in anything other than making money and spending money. Seeing this side of him was refreshing. He seemed to be really into this new lady as he continued to talk about her.

John had been the wild child growing up. As the youngest of four, he got away with everything. There was an 8-year age difference between John and Melissa, and by the time John came along, their parents seemed to be tired of parenting and just let him run wild. With the oldest three, their parents were stern but loving and fun.

"I'm really impressed with Ms. Hammond's work and professionalism. She was very thorough and was able to answer every question before it was even asked. She has a great business mind. How is she doing?" Morgan directed the question to Grant.

"What do you mean? Why would I know? You talk to her more than I do," Grant answered. He had told John a few things about their relationship, or lack thereof. But, he had not talked with Morgan about anything; and John usually kept everyone's secrets.

"I just assumed you were using all of your charm to get the woman to go on a date with you. From the first meeting, it didn't seem you would back down," Morgan smiled and cast his fishing line into the water.

Morgan was right; he knew his siblings very well. Grant hadn't stopped trying to pursue Kaleigh. In fact, he was excited about how far he had come with getting her to go out with him.

"He hasn't backed down. As a matter of fact, he double-downed. He's got her looking for a house. Grant is putting down roots," John laughed.

"You *were* my favorite brother. You usually keep other people's business to yourself," Grant said, with a slight bit of amusement and anger to his voice.

"Ms. Hammond is a beauty, but she doesn't come off as someone who will fall for your handsome good looks and perfect smile. She seems to be very focused on growing her company," Morgan said.

"Her company does mean a lot to her. I gather it's the only thing she has ever had away from her sisters. She's also hiding something about her health," Grant divulged too much information and said the last part mostly to himself.

"How many dates have you been on?" John asked.

"Not many, really. She has had a few health scares around me, and a few other issues I found out from the ER doctor. Headaches, passing out, and chest pains. All very sporadic and seem to come out of nowhere." Grant said that trying to will himself to understand her symptoms.

He told himself he invaded her privacy because he wanted to help. Now, his concern was more than medical. He sincerely wanted to find out what was going on with her and be the person she turned to when she needed help.

"Grant? Are you listening?" Morgan asked.

"Yeah, what were you saying?"

"Dad is on a business trip; he won't make it to the groundbreaking ceremony. Mom will be here today, and she is expecting you to come by for dinner. If you are serious about Ms. Hammond, I think you should invite her over."

"I don't need Mom to approve my dates."

"No, you don't need her to, but you know you want her to. She has a near-perfect track record with our dates."

Their mother was accurate with her first impressions of the women and men her children brought around. In the beginning, none of the siblings wanted her to be right. They wouldn't listen to her assessments of their dates. She had even told Grant to run far away from Hannah. But after a few instances when she was spot on, they became believers.

Grant wasn't sure it was time to introduce his mother to Kaleigh. They were taking things very slowly, and if his mother thought what he was thinking, she would make it her mission to get involved. Whether he wanted them to meet or not, didn't matter; his mother would meet her at the groundbreaking ceremony.

"Well, I have another problem. Hannah is here," Grant announced.

John started choking, and Morgan's expression gave nothing away.

"Hannah? What does she want?" John angrily asked.

"I don't know, but she has already caused trouble. She had a run-in with Kyna."

John asked, "Who is Kyna?"

"Kyna is Kaleigh's sister…the nurse that works for me."

Grant waited for Morgan to say something. He knew his brother would have something to input.

"This is new information. Your girlfriend's sister is one of your nurses? Man, you really know how to pick them," Morgan said, underhandly referring to Grant's bad decisions with women, including Hannah.

"I didn't know they were sisters until well after the meeting with Kaleigh."

"This just gets better and better. So what did Hannah do? I'm sure it was over the top, and she had to show off her manicure." John imitated how Hannah looked at her nails when she was bored or being dismissive.

"Said she just wanted to talk. About what, I don't know."

"Has the sister told Kaleigh yet?" Morgan asked.

"I don't know. She said she would as soon as she saw her. I'm sure it has been spread to all the sisters by now. I begged her for a few days, but I don't think she will wait. Their sibling bond is stronger than ours," Grant sighed, reeling his fishing line back in.

Grant suddenly felt his life slowly spinning out of control. The last time he felt this way, Hannah was the center of it. Now, she was back, and he had no idea what she wanted. Hannah's history was attaching herself to wealthy families. Grant could only speculate that now she was no longer married, she must have thought she could re-attach herself to the Hawkins family.

"Whatever she wants, I don't want to be a part of it. She is a master manipulator, and hearing her name just stresses me out." Grant cast his line into the water again.

"Do I need to get someone to take care of it?" Morgan asked.

When Morgan says, "take care of it," he means a private detective and surveillance, maybe even brute force if necessary. Their big brother remembered the months of terror that Hannah caused, and he would go to any length to get her out of their lives again.

"No, I will handle her," Grant assured him.

"Yeah, you do that," John added. He remembered those months too. If she had been successful, Hannah could have ruined everyone's life.

"Now what is that supposed to mean?" Grant turned to his brother.

"You did a bang-up job last time, and now she's back," John stated the obvious.

Grant turned to stand in front of his brother, "Say what you've got to say, John. You think I still have feelings for her? You think I'm too weak where she is concerned, don't you?"

Grant had heard it all before. John always thought he opened his heart too fast to the women he became involved with. But, when Grant fell in love, he loved hard. Yet, after every heartbreak, he never stopped trying to find the love of his life. Kaleigh may be the one, and she was so different from every other woman he dated.

"I didn't say any of that, but maybe you are feeling that way," John countered, standing toe to toe with Grant.

Morgan's calm voice was raised to get their attention, "Boys, let's calm down. No one is to blame for the acts of that vicious woman."

The brothers were in a heated stand-off. Hannah's antics from years ago almost caused Morgan to lose his business, and the brothers stopped talking for months. Her accusations and drama drew unnecessary attention and bad publicity for their family.

Grant started packing up his equipment. "Listen, the fish aren't biting. If we get back now, I may still have time to make it to church."

"Yeah, let's pack it up. Nothing happening here today. But, I think I will pass on going to church." Morgan followed, packing up his gear.

"Can I tag along with you to church?" John asked, apparently releasing his temporary anger with his brother. He couldn't stay mad with his brother for long.

"Really? Why?" Grant asked, not believing John wanted to hear the word.

"You know what they say about church girls. I just want to check it out," John said with a grin.

"He will never change," Morgan and Grant said in unison.

Grant and John arrived at church in time for the last song of praise and worship. Just as Grant hoped, Kaleigh was leading the worship song.

"Hey, I didn't know your girlfriend could sing. She really has some chops."

Grant barely heard what John was saying. He was engrossed in the music and how beautifully Kaleigh was singing "Encourage Yourself" by Donald Lawrence. Grant felt she was not only singing that to him, but also to herself.

They found a seat in the rear of the church and enjoyed the remainder of the service. The pastor's sermon was about having patience. Pastor Martin started his sermon with a story of how he met his wife and how long he waited for her to say yes to their first date. Their story sounded oddly familiar, and Grant inwardly laughed at himself.

If there were signs in life, this sermon was one of them. With no other woman, did he have the patience that he was clearly experiencing with Kaleigh?

"God has patience with us. The motivation for patience is the redemption of man. We bear the fruit of patience when we, first, trust God's timing. God was preparing me to be the husband my wife needed and preparing her to be the wife I needed. When we first met, we weren't ready. It wasn't our time.

Second, we have to see the big picture. I remember the first time I told my wife about me going back to school. Her face turned bright red; she thought I was crazy. All of this debt we have, and you want to add to it. I didn't talk about it anymore, because she wasn't ready. God was still preparing us. We couldn't see the big picture.

Thirdly, use our wait wisely. She didn't know I received scholarships to go back to school. I didn't have to pay anything out of my pocket. But, that was because I waited, and we waited until God said move. If you don't believe me, open your bible and turn to Psalm 27:14. 'Wait on the Lord, be strong, and take heart and wait for the Lord.' Let's stay in Psalm and go to chapter 37 and verse 7. 'Be still before the Lord and wait patiently on Him: do not fret when people succeed in their ways when they carry out their wicked schemes.'"

Grant immediately pulled out his cellular phone and began taking notes. That last scripture hit home with him and his current situation. As soon as the pastor said, "wicked schemes," he thought of Hannah. She was up to something, and all he had to do was wait and see what she was up to. Just the same with Kaleigh–be patient and trust God's timing.

While John was checking out the ladies throughout the sanctuary, Grant continued to take notes from the sermon. Grant didn't have time to think about his brother and all the ways he was wrong for thinking lustful thoughts in the house of the Lord; he was too busy thinking of ways to prepare himself for a future with Kaleigh.

After service, Grant tried several times to walk towards Kaleigh and her sisters. Each attempt was thwarted by a member of the church introducing their daughter, granddaughter, nieces, and mentees to him and his brother. By the time he was saying goodbye to the first lady of the church, Kaleigh and her sisters were nowhere to be found.

It was just his luck because he was sure Kyna was going to tell Kaleigh about Hannah at the hospital yesterday. Kaleigh finding out was inevitable. Her reaction to the information and what happened afterward would be when Grant needed to exhibit more patience.

Chapter 10

Goosebumps appeared up her arms, and a sudden feeling of her heart dropping wasn't the Holy Ghost Kaleigh was feeling as she sang. She instinctively knew that Grant was in the church somewhere. She sensed his presence before she saw him sitting at the back of the sanctuary with his brother.

Kaleigh knew Grant had heard her sing before, but this time, she wanted to impress him. She was singing one of her favorite songs, and with Grant in the pews, the song meant something a little different this time.

She gave her all to the song, and the musicians simply followed her lead. By the end, the church members were on their feet, crying and shouting. The emotion that took over her was felt by every member sitting in the church.

The pastor took another 15 minutes to get control of the spirit-filled congregation. Pastor Martin preached about patience and when he quoted *Isaiah 40:31, "But they that wait upon the Lord shall renew their strength; they shall mount up with wings as eagles; they shall run, and not be weary, and they shall walk, and not faint. (KJV),"* Kaleigh knew she had the strength to continue on. She applied today's verse to her own life. Dealing with her health issues and trying to run a business had her feeling stressed out. But, she was comforted in knowing she had renewed strength in waiting on God.

After the service, lots of people were hanging around the sanctuary—more than usual. Kaleigh wanted to find Grant and talk to him, but she was continuously being showered with praise for her rendition of the song she ministered. A few members told her they felt her truth coming through the words. Kaleigh wasn't sure what that meant, but she accepted their appreciation.

Once the sanctuary cleared, Kaleigh realized Grant and his brother were gone. She felt disappointed that she didn't get a chance to speak with him. She had finally accepted her feelings and wanted to talk to him, but it would have to wait for another time.

Like every other Sunday, Kaleigh was in her mother's kitchen preparing for their family dinner. She was still thinking of Grant when her phone began buzzing in her pocket. She took a towel from the counter, wiped her hands clean before pulling the device out, and checking her messages. She smiled when she saw a missed call and two text messages from Grant. Poe eased away from her sisters into her father's office before responding to his text messages.

-Saw you in church today. You sang beautifully
-And you looked just as stunning

-Thank you

-I need to talk to you, call me please

-At dinner with family

-Can you get away?

"Poe, who are you texting and smiling at like that?" Karmyn asked.

She quickly slipped her phone into her pocket and turned to Karmyn. "What? Can't I just be happy?"

"Yeah, right. Mom said for us to set the table…dinner is almost ready."

"Okay, I'm coming," Kaleigh tried to suppress another smile.

From the dining room, she heard her mother say, "We don't have all day, Poe."

Kaleigh would have to wait until after dinner to respond to Grant. Her sisters were too preceptive, and she wasn't ready to expose her real feelings for Grant to them or around her parents.

Before the sisters could begin to question her about her health or Grant, Kaleigh started the conversation.

"Karleigh, when is Simon due back?" Her soon-to-be brother-in-law was away at a conference for youth mentoring, where he was a guest speaker. This was the first Sunday since their engagement that he wasn't in attendance for the family dinner.

"I'm going to the airport in two hours. I miss him so much," Karleigh gushed.

"Ugh, really," Kyna faked gagged. "You two make me sick. At least all the wedding plans are done. When do our dresses arrive?"

"The dresses will be here in two weeks. Can you believe it, in just a few months, I will be a married woman," Karleigh squealed like a schoolgirl.

Poe couldn't help being happy and excited for her sister. This is the first wedding for the sisters. Karmyn's marriage to former NFL player, Vincent Gallagher, was an elopement in Las Vegas when he signed his first contract. Her grandmother didn't let her live that down for at least two years.

As the family continued to talk about Karleigh's upcoming wedding, Poe kept thinking about Grant. She wondered what he wanted to discuss. Was he going to ask on her on another date? Or maybe he wanted to talk about taking their relationship to the next stage. The self-doubt started to seep in when she thought that, possibly, he only wanted to talk about finding a house for him, and merely wanted them to stay on the friend level. They had been getting along so well in the past few weeks, but she had kept him at a distance to protect herself.

She didn't want to be presumptuous, but she hoped that he was still interested in her romantically. Poe was ready to move beyond friends and hoped he was still as interested in her. Unknowingly, she started smiling, just thinking of the possibilities.

"There she goes, again," Karmyn said.

"What?" Karleigh asked

"Poe has been smiling like that since she saw Dr. Hawkins in church this morning."

Poe dropped her smile, but only a fraction before it returned. Maybe it was time for her family to know that she was happy. Why was she hiding this from her family? Mostly because she was just accepting and understanding her true feelings.

"Leave your sister alone. She deserves some happiness," her mother said and smiled.

Kyna was unusually quiet, and their grandmother took notice. "Kyna, something on your mind?"

"Nothing, I'm just happy for my sisters," she responded. "I'll start the dishes." Kyna stood and began clearing the table.

Quietness was not one of Kyna's characteristics. The sisters looked from one to another and knew something was wrong. After they cleared the dishes and cleaned the dining room and kitchen, the sisters would definitely have a talk with Kyna.

Usually, after dinner, the sisters would hang out around their childhood home and watch movies with their parents and grandmother, or they would part ways if they had other activities to attend. Kyna tried to leave quickly after they finished cleaning the kitchen, but Karleigh caught her by the wrist and practically dragged her into the basement.

"What do you want?" Kyna asked, clearly agitated by the confrontation. She remained standing near the stairs, looking ready for an easy retreat.

"What's going on with you? You've been quiet, and that's not like you. Now talk," Karleigh demanded, standing behind the bar, taking the wine glasses from the cabinet.

Kyna looked around and got no sympathy from Poe or Karmyn. Poe was just as eager to find out what was going on.

"So, you planning to hold me, hostage, until I talk?" Kyna asked.

All three sisters said in unison, "Yes."

"Fine. But, Poe, you might want to sit down." Kyna grabbed a glass of wine after Karleigh filled one for each of them.

"Why me?"

"Because this has to do with Grant."

Poe got nervous, biting her bottom lip like she used to do when she was a young girl. She had been on cloud nine about Grant and wasn't sure she wanted to hear anything Kyna was about to say.

"I don't think I want to hear it," Poe whispered.

"Have you talked to Grant since Friday?" Kyna asked.

"He brought me lunch and then said he had something special planned for me, but then got pulled away for work." Poe took a sip of wine and sat on the sofa. Karmyn followed behind her and sat down.

"Yeah, the medical director had him fill-in at the community festival we were having. That was kind of my fault. I didn't know you all had plans." Kyna paused before asking again. "But, did he talk to you about the events of that afternoon?"

"No, he texted me after church and said we need to talk. You know what it's about, don't you?" Poe asked.

"Yes. Grant asked me to give him time, and I tried until y'all just ambushed me."

Karmyn was getting frustrated, "Kyna, just spit it out."

"Okay, a woman showed up at the hospital Friday. She was all over him and said she was his fiancée. He tried to push her away."

Poe didn't want to hear anymore, but as Kyna told her what happened, she couldn't stop the tears from falling. Less than eight hours ago, she was getting those good butterfly feelings in her stomach from just seeing him in church. Now, she was getting nauseous thinking about how she wanted to move their relationship to the next level. He had done nothing but lie to her.

"So, that's why you are trying to run out of the house so fast. So, you could give Grant a few more hours to come up with some kind of lie to tell me. You're on his side now?" Poe accused her sister.

"Seriously, Poe. If I were on his side to lie to you, I would have never told you. You know better than that," Kyna spat.

Poe's mind was spiraling. She knew her sister would never hurt her. The fact that the idea even occurred to her was evident that Grant had gotten too close. She could hear Karleigh and Karmyn asking more questions, but their voices were faded into the background.

"How could I be so stupid? I let him get close…too close."

"Hey, don't do that," Karmyn admonished her. "Don't beat yourself up. He fooled us all," Karmyn hugged her, providing some much-needed comfort.

"Wait, if you haven't talked to him, then you don't know what's true. We are only speculating." Karleigh tried to rationalize with her sisters.

"Are you saying I didn't see what I saw?" Kyna asked.

"No, I'm saying it's not always as cut and dry as it may have appeared," Karleigh turned to Poe. "Talk to him and find out the truth."

"You mean the lies. I don't think I have it in me to resist his charm if he tries to deflect."

"You don't give yourself enough credit. I have a better suggestion." Kyna continued when Poe turned to face her. "Let's get to the woman first. I got a bad vibe from her. And like I said, he did try to push her away. A few times."

Kyna could be vindictive and petty sometimes, especially when someone hurt a member of her family. She wasn't someone you wanted to entangle with when she got mad.

"When is the groundbreaking for the new hotel?" Karmyn asked, ignoring Kyna.

"It's Thursday morning. I'm sure he will be there," Poe solemnly answered. She wasn't sure four days would be enough time to mask her feelings for him when they saw each other again.

"Okay, I have a plan," Karleigh suggested. "Poe, continue to ignore him. Let's see what he does once he knows or, at least, believes you know about this woman. Then, let's see how he reacts at the ground-breaking ceremony. A lot can be determined by his actions."

"Sounds like playing games. I don't like it. I just want to be done with him," Poe sat back and took a huge gulp of her wine.

"Unfortunately, Poe, you have a business relationship with his family's company. You will see him from time to time," Karleigh said, refilling her glass.

"And I have to work for him. Even if I wanted a transfer, I probably wouldn't get it," Kyna added.

Poe thought about everything her sisters said. They had all been through different issues with men in their past. Different experiences affect people in different ways. For this situation, Poe felt it best to stay away from Grant for the next few days until she could figure out the best way to deal with her feelings and him in her own way.

"Sisters, thank you for your love and support, but I think I will handle this my way. Kyna, I don't want you to say anything to Grant. You can let him know you told me about the woman. Other than that, let it go. I'll see you all on Thursday at the ground-breaking." Poe sighed, then took a deep, cleansing breath and released it. She squared her shoulders back and held her head high. "I'll be fine, and I will take care of this."

The sisters hugged one another and headed in separate directions. Poe was the first to leave, and instead of going home, where she was sure Grant would be looking for her, she doubled back to her parents' house after she knew her sisters were gone.

She sat in her car for over an hour, in her parents' driveway, looking at the house where she grew up. She thought about all of the homes she showed to Grant and how he seemed to lean on her expertise and opinions about each dwelling. Poe replayed every single encounter they had since they met several months ago in her office. His response to her, his reactions, his interest never seemed to change.

In the past few months, she enjoyed being with him, and he never seemed to pressure her for more than the friendship she was offering. Then Poe began thinking about her parents' relationship. After being married for 35 years, they seemed happy. They had a connection that seemed unbreakable. That was the feeling she was having with Grant; an unbreakable bond was forming. She knew what she had to do, but she didn't like it.

Chapter 11

The past four days had felt like the longest days in Kaleigh's life. She sent Grant a text message that simply said, "I know. I need time." Instead of going into the office and risk Grant coming there looking for her, she decided to work from a bed and breakfast a few towns away. She didn't want Grant to be able to find her if she stayed anywhere nearby.

Running from the situation seemed to work better for her, rather than facing the problem head-on. Kaleigh turned her phone off and only communicated with her office through emails. She instructed Janice to handle all phone calls and distribute any new clients to the other agents.

Unfortunately, today, there was no way to avoid seeing Grant. The ground-breaking for the new Hawkins Hotel was a huge event for the city. The mayor and governor would be in attendance, along with most everyone of any influence in the state. After the ceremony, the Hawkins family would host a private reception for a few investors and government officials to say thank you.

Kaleigh was able to invite her own guests, and of course, her sisters were on the list, along with Karleigh's fiancé, Simon, and his best friend and attorney, Nicolas Butler.

If being in Grant's presence didn't cause Kaleigh any anxiety, being around Nicolas and Karmyn would. They hated each other and never failed to let everyone around know. Both of them were closed-lip about the reason they hated each other, leaving others to formulate their own ideas.

The event planner for the groundbreaking ceremony was ever the professional and escorted Kaleigh to the waiting area set aside for the Hawkins family and other VIP's. She looked around and noticed Grant wasn't there, allowing her to relax and release a breath she didn't realize she was holding. Karmyn and Karleigh had arrived and were talking to Melissa Hawkins and an older woman who was just as beautiful as Melissa. Immediately, Kaleigh realized that the woman must be Mrs. Hawkins, Grant's mother.

"Ms. Hammond, are you just as excited for today as I am?" Morgan asked.

Kaleigh jumped slightly when he approached but recovered quickly. She needed to stay professional and not let her emotions take control.

"Mr. Hawkins, my excitement is barely contained. And please, call me Kaleigh."

"Only if you call me Morgan."

"Deal." Kaleigh gave him a genuine smile. He effortlessly put her at ease, just like Grant would. It must be a family trait.

"I see your sisters are getting along well with my mother and sister. Should we join them?" Morgan extended his hand to her.

"Sure, why not?" She placed her hand in his, and he gently wrapped her hand around his arm. She could feel his muscles through his suit jacket. Grant was also muscular and toned, but not as bulky as Morgan. She silently admonished herself for continually thinking about Grant.

"I must warn you, my mother is an inquisitive old lady. Don't let her badgering bother you." Kaleigh laughed along with Morgan as they walked to the group that now included John, Simon, and Nicolas.

"So much beauty in one place. I must be in heaven," John announced once Kaleigh joined the group.

"My son, the charmer," Mrs. Hawkins laughed.

Up close, Mrs. Hawkins was even more beautiful. Her skin was flawless, and she wore very little make-up. Her hair flowed in long grey tresses down her back and across her shoulders.

"Mrs. Hawkins, it's a pleasure to meet you. I'm Kaleigh Hammond of K. Hammond Realty," Kaleigh reached her hand forward.

"Honey, I know who you are." Mrs. Hawkins clasped Kaleigh's hand within her own, briefly shaking and then releasing. "You and your sisters are absolutely stunning. If I didn't know any better, I would think you all were triplets."

"We have another sister and have been mistaken as quadruplets," Kaleigh corrected her.

"Oh yes, the nurse who works with Grant. I do hope they both arrive soon. Apparently, they had an emergency this morning at the hospital."

Kaleigh kept the same smile and expression plastered to her face, even though her sisters were openly staring at her when Mrs. Hawkins mentioned Grant. Did they think she would start crying at the mention of his name?

"I'm sure Grant will be here soon," Morgan stated, filling the awkward silence. "John, Melissa," He addressed his siblings. "The mayor and governor are here; let's go greet them. Ladies, gentlemen, we must make our rounds. Business first, party second." The siblings left the group leaving their mother behind to continue speaking with The Hammond sisters.

"Kaleigh, Morgan tells me you were very thorough with your research, and your knowledge of historical buildings is impressive. I also hear that you are helping Grant to find a house here. I'm so glad he has decided to stay in one place and plant some roots. I thought he would never settle down."

Karmyn started to cough a little at the mention of settling down. Kaleigh wondered if his mother was referring to the fiancée that suddenly showed up or something else. She didn't know how much his mother knew about her relationship with Grant. Thinking that she may know her son's intent where she was concerned made the moment more awkward than before.

"Okay, Let's get to the ceremony," Karleigh came through with the save.

The ceremony was about to begin. The mayor and governor arrived together, followed by members of the city council and a few influential city leaders. The program would kick off with a few words from the governor, and then the mayor. Pastor Martin would give a prayer to symbolically bless the land, then Morgan would provide a statement before the key players grabbed their shovels and simultaneously crack into the earth.

Just as Pastor Martin stepped up to the podium, Grant tip-toed onto the riser from the right side, and an unknown woman eased on the podium from the left. She was beautiful in a made-up kind of way. Kaleigh thought her make-up was too thick, and her appearance was evident that she was always picture ready.

A tent had been erected for the ceremony, and Kaleigh stood in the back away from everyone. She was able to see the entire stage from her vantage point. Her heart dropped when she saw Grant arrive. He was looking good as usual in a tailor-made grey suit and royal blue tie. The tie was his favorite; he had mentioned it was a gift from his father when he graduated from medical school.

Kaleigh loved how he was close to his family. His relationship with his siblings reminded her so much of her relationship with her sisters. She couldn't help but smile when she thought of the stories Grant told her about growing up with his siblings. The smile didn't last long when Kaleigh noticed the unknown woman who continued to inch closer and closer toward Grant.

Pastor Martin asked everyone to close their eyes and bow their head as he began with his prayer. The prayer ended in a collective

"Amen," and when Kaleigh opened her eyes, the unknown woman was standing right next to Grant. The strained look and the forced smile on Grant's face along with the scowl John was making at the woman told Kaleigh everything she needed to know. This was the mystery fiancée of Grant's.

Kaleigh watched as Grant tried to take steps away from her, and John attempted to step between them. The woman was aggressive and continued to stand close to Grant and, at one point, tried to hold his hand, which he swiftly swatting away.

"So, that's the woman he was engaged to? Doesn't hold a candle to you," Karleigh whispered in her ear. Kaleigh didn't react. She just kept her gaze steady and tried to pay attention to what Morgan was saying.

"His body language is clearly saying he doesn't want to be anywhere near that woman. Karleigh was right. You need to get the entire story," Karmyn whispered from the other side.

Her sisters meant well, but Kaleigh knew her relationship with Grant was better as just friends and nothing more. No matter how she felt about him, he was out of her league. Watching him stand with his billionaire family continued to drive the nail into the coffin.

After the event, Kaleigh watched Grant grabbed the woman by the wrist and drag her away from the party. She made a mental note that he didn't grab her hand but her wrist. That action seemed odd to her.

The media was packing up their equipment, preparing to leave, and the caterers were putting the finishing touches on the brunch buffet when another problem presented itself. A clearly drunk Carl Atwater walked right up to Morgan and John, who was still standing on the stage.

Whatever he was saying was clearly making the brothers upset. Carl started getting loud, which caused Simon and Nicolas to approach the scene. Unexpectedly, John hauled off and punched

Carl square in the face. Kaleigh blinked, and John was being hauled in one direction, and Carl was being pushed in another.

"What's going on?" Melissa asked Kaleigh. Melissa had been talking with the event planner and caterer when the brief altercation happened.

"I don't know, but it's not good, and I know it has something to do with me," Kaleigh solemnly answered her.

Due to the commotion, Grant returned with that woman right on his heels. She seemed to be the clingy type, and Kaleigh despised women like that. How could Grant be attracted to a woman like her? She then apologized to herself for having those thoughts. Kaleigh didn't know this woman from Eve; she could very well be a wonderful person.

"Ugh, why is she here? I thought we got rid of her years ago," Melissa said aloud, then turned to Kaleigh. "Kaleigh, I know my brother likes you a lot. That woman is trouble, and Grant wants no part of her."

"I thought they were engaged," Kaleigh asked her directly.

"They were engaged a few years ago. She tried to destroy his relationship with us and then tried to destroy him, all for money. She is nothing but trouble; causes drama everywhere she goes. I'll let Grant tell you everything, just promise me, when you two do talk, listen to him no matter how outrageous the story may sound."

Karleigh and Karmyn approached Kaleigh just as Kyna was heading in her direction. Kyna had stayed in the back watching the scene unfold.

"Poe, I think you may need Nicolas for this," Karleigh told her.

"Nicolas! Why?"

"Ms. Hammond, we need to go inside," Morgan used his authoritative voice, which indicated he was not to be questioned, at least not out in the open.

Melissa stayed in the tent to continue engaging the guests and ease the fears of the mayor who looked on with concern. Kaleigh's sisters, along with Simon and Nicolas, decided to stay outside and let her handle business with Morgan for herself.

Inside of the soon-to-be hotel lobby, Kaleigh gathered with Morgan and John.

"What is going on?" She asked.

"Kaleigh, I suggest you contact your attorney and possibly a public relations firm as soon as possible. Carl Atwater is making accusations that the Hawkins Group used K. Hammond Realty to cover up an illicit affair you were having with Grant while he was engaged to Hannah Sinclair."

Kaleigh felt the blood drain from her body. She felt light-headed and capable of collapsing at any moment. This woman was out to get Grant and take her down in the process. This couldn't be happening to her. With everything that Kaleigh had to deal with, this woman should be the least of her troubles.

"I'm so confused. How does Carl even know this woman?" Kaleigh asked.

"Hannah is very duplicitous. She wants something," John answered her, clenching his jaw. Kaleigh was glad she was not the cause of the murderous glare John was giving.

"Our family has a history with her. When Grant tried to end the engagement, she attempted to take down our family company. Even though she had recently married an Italian billionaire. She thought she would be able to keep Grant while married to another man." Morgan supplied a little more detail that Melissa had previously offered.

"We thought we were rid of her, but she showed up a few weeks ago," John interjected.

"This is too much. I don't need this in my life. You closed on this building, our business affiliation is done." Kaleigh threw her hands in the air. "Please, just leave me alone." She ran from the building to her car. She didn't acknowledge the cries from her sister or Simon calling after her. She didn't see or hear anything.

Fumbling with her key fob, she was able to open the door and drive off, barely able to see the road through her tears.

*****

Grant saw Kaleigh run from the building, then saw his brothers exit just behind her. He immediately advanced on his brothers. "What did you say to her? What happened?"

"Ask Hannah," John stalked off in an angry huff.

"Morgan? You better talk to me," Grant demanded.

"It looks like Hannah has enlisted the help of Carl Atwater in her little game."

"Carl Atwater? The real estate agent that used to work for Kaleigh?"

"One and the same. He is threatening to leak a story that you had an affair with Kaleigh, which is why you ended your engagement with Hannah. Then, we used her realty firm to find our new hotel as some type of payoff."

"That's ridiculous? Who would even believe such a crazy story?" Grant ran his hand over his head. "I didn't even know her when I was engaged to Hannah. I didn't live here and wasn't even thinking about a residency here at the time."

This had to be the worst timing. Grant could only imagine what Kaleigh could be thinking. He needed to talk to her. He reached into his jacket pocket for his phone to call her but saw a text message from her first.

Don't bother calling or texting me. I don't want to hear it. Just leave me alone.

When Grant took Hannah away from the ceremony, to get her to understand that there would never be anything between them again, she simply laughed in his face and walked away. She said she always gets what she wants, and she wanted him. Well, now, he had three problems; get rid of Hannah, get Kaleigh back, and deal with Kyna, who was currently stomping in his directions.

"What did you do to my sister?" Kyna yelled. Her other sisters were not far behind her, wearing the same concerned look as Kyna. Before Grant could answer, she continued, "I told you to be careful with her. I told you to tell her the truth. Poe is not like the women you date. She is special."

"Don't you think I know how special she is? Kyna, I promise, I didn't want to hurt Kaleigh. I didn't know Hannah would show up today or last week. But, I'll try my hardest to make this right. With her and with you," Grant promised.

"Well, you will have to do this on your own. No help from me at all." Kyna pointed her finger into Grant's chest.

"Grant won't need any help. I think he knows what to do," Morgan said, making his presence known.

Kyna rolled her eyes, then scanned Morgan from head to toe.

"Nurse Kyna, this is my brother, Morgan," Grant offered an introduction.

Kyna ignored Morgan and focused her eyes back on Grant. "You've got some work to do. Good luck." She stormed off with her sisters right behind her.

"Whoa! She is a spitfire. You have to work with her every day?" Morgan rubbed his hand over his bald head.

"She is the smartest and most competent nurse I have ever had. And she pulls no punches."

Grant and Morgan returned to the reception. Amazingly, no one made it known that there was ever a problem. Melissa had the event under control, and before long, Morgan was joking with the mayor. Grant remained distant and off into his own thoughts. Kyna was right; he had some work to do.

Later, the Hawkins family retired to their hotel suite. After the morning they had, relaxation was needed for everyone. Morgan was on a business call, John was sitting at the table eating room service, and Melissa had gone to her room to take a nap.

"Grant, stop biting your lip. You used to do that all the time when you were deep in thought. What's going on with you?" his mother asked.

"Mom, I really messed up this time." Grant moved closer to his mother and placed his head on her shoulder, just like he used to do as a child. "Hannah is playing some kind of game with me to win me back, I guess. And this Carl guy is trying to ruin Kaleigh's business."

"Have you prayed about this?"

If he were honest with himself, he hadn't prayed about anything in a long time. Sure, he had been going to church pretty regularly, but that was in part due to Kaleigh. She made him want to be a better man and a better Christian.

Grant admitted to his mother that he had not been diligent in his prayers. Instead of the lecture, he thought was coming about prayer; his mother flipped the script.

"Hannah has plenty of skeletons in her closet. Find that big bone, the femur bone; wave it in the air, and don't be afraid to hit her with it. And don't forget to pray about it," she laughed. "As for that, Carl guy, maybe Kaleigh or someone in her office, has some insight into his motivation."

"Kaleigh isn't talking to me," Grant admitted

"So, talk to the people in her office. Be discreet. See what they say. Continue to be patient with Kaleigh, I'm sure she didn't have this type of drama in her life before you came around," his mother continued. "This is probably the only time you will hear me say this," she whispered. "Use Morgan's guy to help you. I don't always agree with his methods, but he gets results."

Grant thought about what his mother said. She was right; he was going to need some additional help. Contacting the receptionist at Kaleigh's office couldn't hurt, and using Morgan's guy had its perks. He smiled at his mother, and for the first time since the ground-breaking, he finally relaxed a little because he had a glimmer of hope.

"Well, son, I think I will wake Ms. Sleepyhead and get her to take me shopping." She stood and adjusted her skirt. "I am so proud of all of my children. I think you all need to settle down, get married, and have some kids, but that's for another day." Grant thought his mother was beautiful at 65 years old, and she was very wise.

Grant left the hotel suite soon after discussing with Morgan what he needed from his guy. Something in Carl Atwater's background had to do with the femur bone in Hannah's closet. He laughed at the thought of his mother's analogy. The next stop for Grant was to do his own research on Hannah Sinclair.

He walked into his condo a few hours later and went straight to his laptop. Grant started scouring the internet for articles or pictures of Hannah. She was a known opportunist, groupie, and gold-digger. She lived for the parties and cameras.

Several hours of searching through international websites and celebrity watch sites, he had no new information. It was 2 o'clock in the morning, and Grant was ready to call it a night. He stood to his full height and stretched with a long yawn.

He heard buzzing in the distance and realized his phone was vibrating. He had forgotten to turn the ringer on after the ceremony.

"What's up, John? It's late," Grant answered when he saw the caller ID.

"Brother, I've got some good news for you. I know what's up with Hannah."

"Do tell," Grant sat down in his chair at his desk.

"It seems Hannah was sued by her last ex-fiancé for embezzling funds from his not-for-profit. She claims she was innocent, but they settled out of court for approximately $200,000. But wait, there's more." John sounded like the late-night infomercials. "Now follow along, it's going to get confusing. Carl Atwater has a gambling problem. He owes over $50,000 to the casinos. He met

Hannah through his sister, who is currently married to Hannah's current boy-toy's brother."

Grant scratched his head, trying to keep up with the details that John was throwing at him. "Wait, say that again?"

"Carl's sister is married to the brother of Hannah's new boyfriend." John tried to clarify.

"Where did you get this information from?" Grant asked.

"Morgan's guy. He couldn't reach you, so he called me."

"I feel like you are about to say there is more," Grant sat back in his chair and used his free hand to rub his head. The information he was hearing was unbelievable.

"You would be right, Kemosabe. Hannah promised Carl the money he needed for his gambling debts if he would help destroy Kaleigh and get you to come back to her. I think she found out about you and Kaleigh through Carl. Anyways, with Kaleigh still mad at you, Hannah thinks her plan is working. Carl's part is simply revenge. He is angry with Kaleigh for making him actually do work in the office. He hated that Kaleigh always assigned him clients instead of letting him find his own. Most of the time, he had to work with her, which to him meant he had to share his commission."

Grant had to digest all that was being relayed to him. It was all sounding too much like a bad soap opera. "So, let's get back to Hannah. Why would she go to all of this trouble to get back with me? She has to know there was no chance of that ever happening, right?"

"Well, she is a spoiled brat, *annnnnddddd…*" John dragged out the word for effect. "She also found out that you are the recipient of a medical research grant."

"How does she know about that; the winners haven't been announced yet. The official announcement isn't made public for another month."

"Well, she knows, and possibly others know, too. Congratulations, bro!"

Grant couldn't really celebrate the most significant accomplishment in his career thus far. Just knowing that Hannah has this information must play into a grander scheme of things she has planned.

Before John's call, he had been ready to call it a night, but now, his energy was revived, and he needed to think outside of the box to find that big bone his mother mentioned.

Hannah couldn't possibly think she would be able to get her hands on any of his research money. So how does knowing this information help her? Grant pondered that question and everything that had happened since her arrival.

Grant awakened hours later with his forehead plastered to the keyboard of his laptop and a pain in his neck from the awkward sleeping position. Immediately, he reached for his cell phone and checked the time. He had missed five calls and several text messages from the hospital, his brothers, Kyna, and his mother. But, none from Hannah. He found that interesting.

Within an hour, Grant showered, dressed, and was on his way to the hospital. He hadn't missed any appointments, and according to the messages, none of his patients were in labor. He had no idea what was going on at the hospital or what was so urgent.

Grant parked his car in his reserved parking place and entered the hospital through the employee parking garage as he would typically do. His route to the gynecology and obstetrics department usually took him past the cafeteria to the elevators near the gift shop and up to the fifth floor. He talked to the barista at the coffee shop as he ordered his cup of coffee and the florist in the gift shop when he stopped by picking up a bouquet for the nurses on shift. Both women seemed different, maybe happier than usual. Grant couldn't put a finger on why their behavior seemed unusual to him.

He continued to his office, offering greetings to a few of the staff he knew. They, too, seemed different. The neo-natal care unit was on the fifth floor, where his office was located. Grant stopped to banter with the nurses in this department on the way to his office, but again, something seemed off to him. They seemed to know something he didn't.

Other department staff and nurses stared and smiled as he walked past. Only a few greeted him in their usual demeanor, but with indescribable joy to their faces. Grant turned toward the nursing station, spread his arms open wide. "What is it? Somebody better tell me something. It's not my birthday."

A few ladies giggled, but he received no response. "OK, play your games." He turned back toward his department and used his key card to open the double doors. As the doors swung open, a throng of people pushed forward, all screaming congratulations!

Grant was shocked but, what surprised him the most was Hannah, leading the charge. Before he could react, Hannah had pulled him into an embrace and kissed his cheek, leaving behind the mark of a seductress. Grant's eyes connected directly with Kyna, but she didn't have a look of disdain on her face. She seemed uninterested or indifferent.

"Dr. Hawkins, we were so excited to find out that you were awarded the prestigious award and grant from the Hollins Foundation," the medical director addressed Grant with a hard slap to the back. We are also grateful to Ms. Sinclair for notifying us of your accomplishment and planning such a wonderful celebration on such short notice."

Grant was unable to speak, looking at the grandeur that Hannah had gone through to make this happen. There were balloons everywhere, a long table full of food and a cake very similar to a wedding cake with three tiers. Most people would be excited about winning the award and ecstatic about having a surprise celebration. But, Grant knew there was more to this party. He wanted to strangle Hannah; instead, he continued smiling and accepting congratulatory handshakes from the nurses and doctors in his department. When Kyna approached, Hannah jumped in front of her.

"Nurse, can you refill the punch bowl? It's over there." Hannah pointed across the room with her perfectly manicured nail.

"No! Now move." Kyna used the back of her hand to move Hannah's finger away from her face.

Grant immediately started sweating. He was concerned that Hannah would cause a scene; she was known for creating and maintaining drama. However, he found solace in knowing that Kyna would not do anything to risk her position with the hospital. She had too much invested to allow Hannah to destroy that. The moment was saved when the medical director joined the trio.

"Hannah, have you met nurse Kyna? Kyna is one of the best nurses in this hospital. She has more letters behind her name than I have," he said with a belly laugh.

"I doubt that," Hannah tried to say under her breath, but the medical director heard her.

"On the contrary, Kyna has a doctorate in nursing and molecular biology," the director beamed with pride. "That's the number one reason why I paired these two together. Their brains are like a match made in heaven." The director laughed again.

Kyna smiled and responded, "Thank you for the compliment. I was just telling Hannah how I am so excited to get started on this research. Especially since the proposal includes 50% of my research. That means plenty of long nights with Dr. Hawkins." Kyna made sure to emphasize long nights while staring intently at Hannah.

"*You're* Dr. Hammond on the grant award?" Hannah swallowed, and the coloring drained from her face. Grant almost laughed out loud because he knew what Hannah might have been thinking. In her quest for revenge, she didn't research all the key players. She had no idea that Dr. Hammond was a woman or the nurse she tried to belittle. In her warped mind, doctors were men, and nurses were women.

Hannah had a superiority and a privileged attitude. She was raised in a family where material possessions were a status of your wealth and worth. Her father was a successful businessman, and her mother was the perfect trophy wife, giving her husband only one child. Her mother taught her to find a rich husband, give him a child, and you would be set for life.

The problem with that logic was Hannah's father knew all about his wife's mission to marry a rich man. When he died, his last will and testament left absolutely nothing to his wife and daughter. Hannah's mother told her it was now her responsibility to make sure they continued to live a life of extravagance.

The standoff between Hannah and Kyna went unnoticed to the director, so Grant took that moment to guide Kyna into an empty exam room where they could talk in private. "Excuse me, Hannah, Dr. Williams; I need to speak with nurse Kyna."

Once inside of the room, Kyna quietly let go of her temper. "Really, Grant, this woman is driving me crazy. She marches in here this morning, with information about the award that the review board hadn't even announced yet."

"Listen, I learned some interesting facts last night, and I need to talk to Kaleigh," Grant pleaded with her.

"She doesn't want to talk to you," Kyna answered, shaking her head.

"Well, I need to speak with Janice. It has to do with Carl Atwater." Grant paced the room, rubbing his hand over his head.

"I can probably get Janice to meet with you. But while I arrange that, you need to get rid of that woman." She plastered on a fake smile and swung the door open, almost striking Hannah.

"He's all yours," Kyna's voice dripped with sugar.

Instead of staying in the room with Hannah, Grant breezed past her and began talking with a few other colleagues, attempting to ignore her presence. Hannah had other plans and tried to stay as close to Grant as possible. He knew she hated being around him when he spoke with his colleagues about medicine. The content went over her head, and she claimed it was mind-numbing talk.

Grant tried to keep the conversations at a high level, which usually bored her, and she would walk away on her own.

An hour later, the crowd had dispersed. Grant tried to sneak away, but Hannah saw him attempting to leave. She followed him as he walked to the elevators.

"I'm sure you're not leaving without me. Aren't you going to thank me?" Hannah asked. She was searching for a compliment or maybe just a conversation. Grant wasn't interested in either.

"For what, Hannah?" he said, gruffly.

"Grant, don't be obtuse. You should thank me for doing all of this to celebrate you."

"And nurse Kyna. Don't forget, this is her research, too." Grant got a kick out of reminding her about that piece of information. And it elicited the reaction he wanted. Hannah's response caused her face to scrunch up like she smelled something foul.

"Well, she can't be too smart if she has a doctorate in nursing. I mean, what do they call her doctor nurse or nurse doctor?" Hannah laughed at herself.

Grant ignored Hannah as she continued talking after stepping into the elevator. Most of it was self-praise for what she considered her best surprise party. The sound of her voice was beginning to grate on his nerves. She sounded akin to fingernails on a chalkboard. He couldn't get away from her fast enough. Amazingly, she was able to keep up with him in her 4-inch stiletto heels.

By the time they reached Grant's car, he had enough of her. He turned abruptly, causing her to lose her footing and stumble backward, "Hannah!" he yelled. "Stay away from me. Me and you, this," he pointed back and forth from his chest to her. "We will never be again. I finally found someone who I can see myself growing old with. A woman whose heart is just as beautiful as her face. And that face doesn't need a pound of Maybelline."

"Grant, you can't mean that!" her smiled faltered.

"I do mean it. I have never meant something so much in my life. I know all about your debt and that of Carl Atwater's. I know about you sleeping with the chairperson over the foundation, presenting me the award and the grant for my research. None of this will get you back into my good graces." For a moment, Grant thought he saw remorse in her eyes, but that was quickly replaced with a devious smile.

Grant continued, "And if I have lost any chance with Kaleigh Hammond, I will make sure you pay where it hurts most. In that designer handbag of yours."

"I thought you were a forgiving, Christian man?" Hannah asked while pouting.

"Even Christians have a limit. But, I do forgive you. I forgive you for everything you have done to my family and for anything you are plotting now. My faith is why I can walk away from you with no hesitation. Goodbye, Hannah."

Grant got into his car, slammed the door, and took a long deep breath before pulling off and leaving Hannah standing stunned in the hospital parking garage.

Chapter 12

The first few weeks after the incident at the groundbreaking, Kyna made several attempts to talk to her sister. Kaleigh had avoided that conversation and any other attempts her sisters had at contacting her. Every morning, she would send a "Good Morning" text, so her sisters knew she was alive. Otherwise, she worked from home and refused to answer the door no matter how long her sisters banged. They respected her space and didn't use the spare key that each of them had. Leaving notes in her mailbox was their way of communicating with her.

Her only solace was that she wasn't having any severe headaches or problems with breathing as of lately. The past few weeks, being away from everyone was making her body feel better. That thought made her sad because she missed Grant. She missed his company and talking to him about anything and everything. That emotional pain was beginning to feel just as bad as the physical pain she had.

Janice and Regina checked in with her every day by email and kept her updated with information on new and old clients, including Dr. Hawkins. Kaleigh learned that Grant submitted a purchase offer on the McCarter house. She loved that house, too. If she could have afforded it, she would have purchased it for herself.

Janice prepared the necessary documents, but Kaleigh would still need to be present at the closing. She knew it was time to face Dr. Grant Hawkins.

The closing was scheduled for 9 a.m. the next morning. Kaleigh was excited for Grant, but still nervous to see him again. Her heart hadn't healed yet. Being in a room with him when she still had feelings for him would be a test of her strength. God had a way of putting her through tests to strengthen her testimony, and this encounter would be no different.

Kaleigh didn't have any more work to distract her for the day and still had the entire afternoon to sulk around the house. Continuing to ignore her sisters' calls, she turned her television on and flicked channels until she saw images of Grant and Kyna on the news station.

Dr. Grant Hawkins and Dr. Kyna Hammond are the recipients of the prestigious Hollins award and grant for medical research. The first African American recipients and the first from Metropolitan Hospital.

Kaleigh dropped into her chair in shock at what the news reporter said. First, she had to grapple with the thought that Kyna was a doctor. When did this happen? The sisters just thought she liked to be alone since there was a gap in their age differences. She would have never thought Kyna was studying to become a doctor. The second thing was that they were the recipients of some research grant important enough o get television recognition. Kaleigh had no idea what type of research it was, but she immediately felt proud of them both.

A single tear dropped at the revelation that Kaleigh had not been there for her sisters. The video segment that accompanied the report seemed to be a recent award ceremony, and everyone was there except for her. She had missed a considerable accomplishment in Kyna's life, and for what?

Suddenly, Kaleigh felt horrible for ignoring calls, emails, and text messages. Her sisters hadn't wanted to console her; they had lives that they wanted her to be a part of. Especially Karleigh, the wedding was getting closer, and she was the maid of honor. Kaleigh had been silent and unavailable when her sisters needed her. She didn't intend to push everyone away; she just needed time to be alone.

Kaleigh tried to call Kyna, then Karmyn. Both calls went to their voicemails. In her haste, she quickly grabbed her keys from the rack, her jacket from the hall closet, and headed for the front door. She swung the door opened and ran smack into Karleigh.

"Dang Sister, where is the fire?" Karleigh laughed.

"Karleigh, I'm so sorry. I shouldn't have locked myself away from the world. I've missed so much. I don't even know where you are with the wedding plans," Kaleigh rambled.

"Slow down, Poe. Yes, you were missed, but we all understood you needed time to be alone. We know you communicated with Janice every day, and we received every text message. That was enough for us. Besides, I have a key." She jingled her key ring in front of her sister.

Poe allowed herself to relax. She had momentarily forgotten that her sisters had a key to her house. If they really wanted to intrude, they could have. Her sisters understood her, and she loved them for it.

"Why are you here now? Has something happened?" They were still standing in the doorway.

"Can I come in first? Geesh!" Karleigh laughed as they both walked through the foyer and into the kitchen. Poe locked the door behind them and followed her sister.

"I figured it was time to get you out of your self-imposed funk. Plus, I need my maid of honor. The dresses have arrived, and I need to finalize some last-minute details. My plan was to drag you from this house if I had to," the sisters laughed together. Poe knew her sister would really drag her from the house.

"Thank you, Sister, for everything." She embraced her sister and embraced the warmth of the love they shared.

The sisters made several stops, one to the decorator and then to the bakery. Their last stop was to the dress boutique, where they met with Kyna and Karmyn. Poe couldn't keep her tears from falling when she saw her sisters. They had been there for her through every good and bad life event. She would always remember that if she ever wanted to lock herself from the world again.

During the dress fitting, they talked about everything that had happened over the past few weeks, but no one brought up Grant or the research award that Kyna received. Poe could feel the sisters tiptoeing around the subject. She decided to broach the topic first.

"Sooo, Kyna. I saw you on television with Grant receiving some kind of award. You looked good, girl. And, when did you become a doctor?"

For a few seconds, no one said anything. It felt like the air was sucked from the room.

"Yeah, I wanted to tell you with everyone else. I've been so distant over the last few years because I was in school. No one knew." Kyna took a sip of her mimosa.

"So, you really are a doctor?" Poe asked, shocked. "I thought the news just got it wrong."

"I have two doctorates and three master's degrees," Kyna proudly said. "Every time I finished one degree, something awesome was happening in one of your lives." She turned to each of her sisters. "I didn't want to overshadow that. So. I kept it to myself."

"Are you addicted to college degrees or something?" Poe asked in jest.

"She is just an overachiever. Not good enough being the baby of the family, but she had to go and become a doctor," Karleigh teased her.

There was another silence, and Poe didn't know what was going on. Her sisters were being distant and not bubbly like they had been just minutes earlier.

"Tell me. Whatever it is, just tell me," Poe demanded.

All eyes turned to Kyna, "I have other news. I didn't want to tell you in a message."

"Spit it out for heaven's sake."

"I got married a few months ago."

Poe jumped up, knocking over a small table with a bottle of champagne. "You did what? Why didn't you tell us?"

Kyna retold the story of her whirlwind romance and the issues they were trying to work through.

"You keep saying him and my husband, who is he?"

Karleigh grabbed the second bottle of champagne, and Karmyn stood up, ready to step in.

"Morgan Hawkins, I didn't want to say anything because mentioning Grant's name around you was fragile," Kyna whispered.

A full minute passed before Poe started hysterically laughing. The other sisters looked at each other and weren't sure if they should laugh or call a psychiatrist.

"You snagged a multi-billionaire, that I happen to be working for and whose brother is pursuing me all in one night." Poe shook her head in disbelief, "We need another bottle of champagne."

The sisters hadn't laughed like that in quite a while. Enjoying one another's company was long overdue. Poe mentally noted that she would never go so long without her sisters again. They needed each other.

"Well, I am so proud of you and Grant, and we can talk later about Morgan," Poe said.

The sisters kept quiet again and just looked back and forth from one to the other.

"Is it okay to talk about Grant? Poe, we don't want you to be upset." Karmyn asked.

"I'm okay. I probably need to talk about him. Talk about the whole situation," Poe responded.

"Have you talked to him since the ground-breaking ceremony?" Karmyn poured herself another mimosa.

"I haven't talked to anyone except for Janice and Regina. I made sure they knew I would fire them if they brought his name up." She giggled at the thought of her threatening her co-workers. "But Janice had to mention him, seeing as he did put an offer on one of the houses I showed him."

"He decided to stay with your company, that was nice of him," Karleigh said.

The room got quiet again. Poe took a deep breath and asked what she wanted to know ever since they arrived at the boutique. "Kyna, how is he?"

Kyna was tight-lipped about Grant. If Poe didn't know better, she would think that Kyna was keeping something from her. Maybe she was. She had kept her education and her research project a secret.

"Sister, I'm here for you, whatever you need from me. But, I have to work with Grant, and I don't want anything to affect either relationship. Please don't make me get involved," Kyna pleaded.

"Dang, Sister, all she asked was how he was doing." Karmyn was shaking her head.

"Okay, he was all messed up over you. And, that woman didn't make it any better. But, if you really want to know, ask him yourself. Aren't you going to see him at the closing tomorrow?"

"I am. I guess I will ask him for myself," Poe responded, taken aback by her sister's rebuff.

"Kyna! What is wrong with you?" Karmyn angrily asked.

"I'm conflicted, okay. I have to work with Grant for the next few years working on this research, and then I have my sister. I've worked my butt off for this research, but I love my sister. I just want to stay out of all of it."

Poe couldn't be mad at her sister. Kyna had a point, she did have to work with him. Putting her in the middle wasn't fair. "Sister, I'm sorry. I would never come between you and your career. Even if I have my issues with Grant." Poe hugged her sister tightly. "Forgive me?"

The sisters continued with their dress fittings and talking about everything. Afterward, they decided to grab dinner and drinks. Karleigh would be getting married in three weeks, and there were still details that needed to be discussed. The bridal shower and bachelorette party had been planned and would take place next week. It seemed like the stress and bridezilla moments that Karleigh put them through were finally coming to an end.

For the first time in weeks, Poe felt good and happy for herself and her sisters.

*****

Grant watched the sisters from across the restaurant. He saw them when they entered, and his heart slammed against his ribs when he saw Kaleigh's smile. She was beautiful and looked healthy. In his calls with Janice, he tried to find out about Kaleigh's health, but Janice was strictly business.

In the past few weeks, Grant wanted to run to Kaleigh and share everything that had happened. At the very least, he wanted to explain about Hannah. Carl Atwater came clean about his association with Hannah and her plans to destroy Grant's life.

Hannah was still angry that Grant didn't fight for her when she ended their engagement. In her sick mind, she was playing a game to see if Grant was worthy. When her game didn't work, she resented Grant for moving on so quickly. Hannah had been seeking revenge ever since. She was having a relationship with a member of the board of the Hollins Foundation. She used that information to get access to Grant and to his hospital. Her plan was to make accusations of infidelity and ethical medical practices against Grant, in turn making the hospital look questionable. Hopefully, then, the foundation would take the funding away, leaving Grant and his nurse looking stupid.

The plan failed when the hospital's medical director, Dr. Williams, called his friends at the foundation to confirm Dr. Hawkins had been awarded the funding. Dr. Williams became cautious about Hannah and had her investigated. While that investigation was happening, the director received confirmation of the award and allowed Hannah to plan the surprise party.

Hannah was later taken into police custody for several charges—one being extortion of the Hollins Group board member. She wouldn't be blackmailing anyone else any time soon.

Grant sat at the end of the bar and continued to watch the sisters. He smiled when they laughed and frowned when it appeared Kaleigh was experiencing discomfort. He knew that look well. She tried to cover it with a forced smile, but he knew she was in pain.

The right thing to do would be to leave, but he desperately wanted to talk to her. He needed to speak to her. He reminded himself to just stay patient; he would get his chance in due time. Grant moved his chair back to stand and bumped into someone. He quickly turned around to apologize.

"Don't even think about it," Kyna held her hands up in front of her.

"Nurse Kyna," he tipped his head toward her and smiled.

"She's enjoying herself right now. You'll see her tomorrow at the closing," she patted his back.

"Patience has never been something I've been good at," Grant admitted. He wanted what he wanted, and he wanted Kaleigh. He had been praying while waiting her out. Tomorrow he would claim what was his.

"Look at her," Kyna instructed him.

"She looks like she is in pain," Grant slightly winced when Kaleigh grabbed her knee.

"I noticed, too. She has been covering it up all day. She still doesn't know what's wrong. The headaches, respiratory issues, allergies, and joint pains. Nothing is adding up."

Suddenly the light bulb in Grant's mind clicked on brightly. "I just thought of something." Grant kissed Kyna on the cheek and grabbed his coat. "I have to go."

Grant raced from the restaurant and headed to the hospital, needing to talk to Kaleigh's rheumatologist. He had an idea of what she was going through and needed to talk it over with the specialist.

The next morning, Grant was whistling a fancy tune. The closing on his new home was planned for 9 a.m., and he was ready to see Kaleigh again. She wouldn't be able to deny him any longer.

He was able to talk with her specialist and confirm what he had been thinking. She would finally have answers. Grant would let her doctor tell her what they discovered. Today, he wanted their meeting to be about their coming to a mutual understanding. He was determined to make Kaleigh listen to him.

Grant arrived at the K. Hammond Realty office a few minutes early, wanting to talk to Janice first. The office seemed quieter than usual. Janice wasn't at her desk, so Grant walked to the first open area and didn't see Regina or Todd. An odd feeling coursed through his body, and he instantly knew something was wrong.

Janice came rushing from Kaleigh's office.

"Oh, Grant, thank God you are here. Come quickly."

Grant rushed behind Janice to find Regina holding Kaleigh in her lap on the floor.

"What happened?"

"She was talking to me about your closing paperwork and then grabbed her chest. I thought she was having a heart attack, and then she said something about her head and passed out."

"Did you call 911?"

"That's what I was coming out to do when I saw you," Janice said.

"Call her sisters," Grant reached down and effortlessly lifted her lifeless body in his arms. "I'll take her to the hospital."

Grant had called ahead to the hospital, meeting Kaleigh's rheumatologist and nurse at the emergency room doors. They assisted with getting her from the car and taking her right inside to a private room. Grant waited for her sisters in the waiting room.

"What happened?" Karleigh and Simon were the first to arrive.

Grant retold the events and then, again, when Karmyn arrived. Kyna texted to say she was on her way and wouldn't be there for a few hours.

After four hours, Kyna came running through the doors. "Any news?"

"Nothing, yet. She is still with the doctors," Karleigh answered.

"Have you called the parentals?" Kyna asked.

"They are on their way back from the church retreat. They said they will wait to hear from us," Karmyn answered.

Grant was sitting in the corner of the waiting room with his head down. Today was supposed to be a good day. He prayed about this day. Grant felt like God was telling him *not yet*, that he wasn't ready. No matter the kind of training you have, nothing prepared you for the sight of seeing someone you love unresponsive.

Even as a skilled physician, Grant was scared when he walked into Kaleigh's office, seeing her on the ground. Now, he was sitting in the waiting room like so many of his patient's family members. Grant jerked his head up and looked around. He could have sworn he heard a voice say patience. The voice was male, and the only other guy in the room was Simon, and he was talking with Karleigh across the room.

Grant closed his eyes and leaned his head back against the wall. He heard the voice again, causing him to sit straight up and open his eyes. Patience.

"It's been hours, why haven't they told us something?" Karmyn asked to no one in particular. She was pacing the room.

"Testing takes a while, sometimes. We just have to be patient," Kyna answered. When Grant heard Kyna say that, he started laughing. It was all around him. God's voice was so clear. *In His time, not my own*, Grant whispered to himself.

"Patient? We have been patient. She has been going through this for months, maybe longer. I'm tired of being patient," Karleigh cried while Simon embraced her.

"We need to be joyful in hope, patient in affliction, and faithful in prayer," Grant said.

"Grant is right," Kyna reached for her sisters' hands. Simon stood with Karleigh, and Karmyn reached for Grant. They formed a circle to begin prayer. Simon started the prayer, but he didn't only pray for Poe, he also prayed for the other families waiting. He prayed over the doctors and nurses, the patients, and the hospital staff. He started giving God thanks for the healing that was already taking place and for being faithful to His word.

Simon's prayer had other people in the waiting room in tears, but it gave Grant a sense of peace he didn't realize he needed. At that very moment, he knew everything would be alright.

A nurse called out to the waiting room, "Ms. Hammond's Family?"

All three sisters responded, "Yes?"

"Your sister asked that you come back now."

Karleigh looked to Grant, eyes full of tears, and whispered, "Thank you" before kissing her fiancé and following the nurse and her sisters into the emergency room.

Simon walked over to Grant and dropped his arm over his shoulder. "Grant, thank you for being there when Poe needed you."

"Right place at the right time," Grant shrugged.

"God's divine intervention. Karleigh has told me about you and Poe. Listen, I went through something similar with Karleigh. Those Hammond sisters are something else. But don't give up."

"I don't plan to."

"I can't believe I am about to ask you this. Those women are really getting to me," Simon laughed. "Can I expect to have some male back-up in this family?"

Grant gave a hearty laugh before responding, "Simon, if I make it through, expect that back-up real soon."

The two men extended hands and embraced in the one-arm guy hug.

Chapter 13

The private hospital room that Grant arranged for Kaleigh ran out of tissue. The sisters had been crying so hard, the nurses came in to check on them a few times. The tears were of sadness, but also of relief. Finally, Kaleigh was diagnosed with having lupus erythematosus. Lupus was an autoimmune disease that mistakenly attacks its own tissue and organs in the body.

Kaleigh had been having the symptoms for years, causing doctors to incorrectly diagnose her with migraines, acid reflux, and arthritis. But now, thanks in part to Grant, Kaleigh had been given the series of testing needed for lupus. Finally, having a diagnosis and a clear understanding of what was happening to her gave Kaleigh a sense of peace. No more guessing and not knowing. Now, since lupus had no cure, they could begin to manage her illness.

Karleigh started praying for her sister; it was a prayer they used to say as kids.

"Dear God, take care of my sisters." Karmyn and Kyna joined in. "When I can't be there, she will know that you are there to protect her, to keep her safe and guide her when she may feel lost. You are not only a heavenly father but a provider, a protector, a healer, and a deliverer."

Kaleigh joined in for the final part of the prayer, "Thank you, Father, for my sisters, who stand for me when I can't stand for myself." Kaleigh then began singing the song they had adopted as their sister song by Pastor Marvin Sapp.

"Never would have made it. Never could have made it without you. I would have lost it all, but now I see how you were there for me."

"I can't believe it has taken this long to find out what is really going on with you. How do you feel?" Karleigh asked.

"I'm not sure. Relieved, but also sad. I mean, I will have to deal with this for the rest of my life, but at least I now know what 'it' is."

"Sister, you are stronger than any of us. This is something that you will overcome," Karmyn told her.

"I know I will. Because I have my sisters, my family, and…" Kaleigh didn't finish the sentence. He had been responsible for the doctors looking into the lupus diagnosis. She finally realized that she needed and wanted Grant in her life.

"Go ahead and say it," Karmyn mocked.

"And Grant. At least I hope Grant still wants to date me after all of this. From the beginning, he has been my hero, saving me here and there. Would he even want to deal with everything I have going on?"

"See, that's that crazy part talking again. Poe, that man has been going crazy trying to figure how to win you back," Kyna claimed.

"But, that was before we knew I have a life-altering, non-curable disease."

"Remember, he is the one who figured it out. Without Grant, an obstetrician I might add, you still may not know," Kyna informed her.

"She's right. I think he's in it for the long haul, Poe," Karmyn added.

Kaleigh didn't have to think over the comments her sisters made. The truth was staring her in the face. Grant had rushed her to the hospital more times over the past few months than anyone else. If he hadn't wanted to be there for and with her, he didn't have to.

"Do you know if he is still here?" Kaleigh eagerly asked.

"He was in the waiting room with Simon when we came back here," Karleigh noted.

"Can you go get him? I don't have my phone." Kaleigh was ready to tell him how she felt. What he did with that information was up to him.

"Well, you may have to wait," Kyna answered. "We just got paged to a delivery. One of our patients just came in. I gotta go, sister." She walked around the bed and gave her sister a kiss

"That's my baby sister; always on the go." The sisters laughed again.

Kaleigh was released later that afternoon after the doctors came in to talk with her about treatments and pain management. Since there was no cure for Lupus, Kaleigh's treatment was based more on improving her quality of life by learning to control her symptoms. She was placed on an anti-inflammatory drug and had to meet with a dietician. She was sensitive to the sun and required to wear sunscreen every day, no matter what. Lupus required a lifestyle change, and Kaleigh was ready for the challenge.

Janice and Regina came by to see her and brought her car with them. Simon wouldn't allow Kaleigh to drive herself home once she was released, so he offered to chauffeur her around for the day. She was a little saddened that she still had not seen Grant. Kaleigh was ready to talk to him, but she had to be patient.

She made the first stop to her parent's house. Her parents were also thankful to have a diagnosis, finally. Kaleigh was told that her great-grandmother also had Lupus, and she lived to be 101 years old.

"Baby, it's not a death sentence. You may not understand it, but God placed this on you because he knew you could handle it," her mother stressed.

Kaleigh understood what her mother was saying. Like the saying, God doesn't give you more than you can bear. Well, Kaleigh was determined not only to endure this storm but also to work diligently to raise awareness for this disease.

After leaving her parent's house, Kaleigh had Simon take her to get a chicken shawarma before taking her home. While she ate, she rescheduled Grant's closing for the next morning and worked on some other things from the office.

She wavered over whether she should text Grant to thank him for being there for her, but she wanted to tell him in person. She had so much she needed to say. Kaleigh hoped that Kyna conveyed her appreciation to him.

The next morning, Kaleigh was feeling a bit fatigued but kept her body moving. She checked her phone for new messages from Kyna or Grant, and there was nothing. That disappointed her briefly. Knowing she would get to see him and talk to him made her feel better.

She took her time easing from the bed and walking into the bathroom to shower. Kaleigh wanted the day to be extra special. Even with a slight headache and some joint pains, she was singing a happy tune.

This is the day, this is the day that the Lord has made. I will rejoice, I will rejoice and be glad in it.

She finally made it into the office a few minutes later than usual. The prescribed drugs weren't working yet, and she still had some joint pains in her ankles and knees. Attempting to balance her purse, a cup of coffee, and some file folders, Kaleigh tried to open the door and nearly dropped everything.

Again, it was Grant to the rescue. "Good Morning, Kaleigh."

His deep voice caused shivering in her bones, and she nearly forgot all about her physical pain. He was all the medicine she wanted.

"Good Morning, Grant." She gazed into his eyes, and her heart melted when he smiled. Kaleigh almost forgot how good Grant looked.

"Let me get the door for you." He reached out to hold the door so she could enter her office.

"Thank you. You can follow me into the conference room. I tried to get here early, but I was a little sluggish this morning." Kaleigh had no idea why she was rambling on.

"I understand." Grant smiled again, and Kaleigh lost her step and tripped over the rug in the hallway. Grant was there to keep her from hitting the ground, but she lost her cup of coffee in the process.

"Let me get you another cup of coffee. Two sugars, no cream, right?"

"Yes," Kaleigh was impressed, he remembered. "Oh, I also wanted to thank you for yesterday. I appreciated you being here and taking me to the hospital," she was rambling again.

Grant grabbed her arms and forced her to stand still. "Kaleigh, we need to talk."

Usually, it was bad news when someone said they needed to talk. She was now second-guessing telling him how she felt. Maybe he didn't feel the same way about her that she felt for him. Maybe Kyna had it all wrong, and he didn't want a relationship with her. She tried not to let her face react negatively to his announcement.

Nervously, she said, "Okay."

They moved into the conference room. Not wanting to be disturbed, Grant locked the door. For a few seconds, both just stared at the floor, not moving or saying a word.

"I have so much I want to say, so much to explain to you. First, I want you to know, I care a great deal about you."

Grant walked over to Kaleigh and removed the file folders from her arms, placing them on the table. He then took his large hands and covered her smaller ones.

Kaleigh smiled, and her heart filled with joy. She wanted to hear him say that, even after everything she had put him through since the first time they met. This moment felt full-circle, being in the conference room where their attraction began. A little glimmer of hope shined through when he said those words.

"I don't know what Kyna has told you about Hannah…"

"Don't, Grant." Kaleigh stopped him from going into detail about that awful woman. "I know everything, but I don't care. She was an obstacle that I let get in the way. I let my lack of self-esteem take a blow because of her, and that will never happen again."

"What are you saying?" he brought her hands close to his face and then briefly kissed her knuckles.

"I'm saying, I care about you, too, Grant. Let's see where this takes us."

*****

Grant wanted to spin her around and plant a kiss on her right then and there. Happiness was an understatement to describe how he felt hearing her say that. He was excited and elated that she felt the same way.

Instead of acting on his first impulse to kiss her, they sat at the conference table and talked. The closing agent called to inform them that he was running late and would be there soon. For over an hour, they talked about developing their relationship. Building it on a foundation rooted in a love of God.

"I didn't want to care about you, and I didn't want to get too close. I knew I was sick, and I didn't think it was fair for you to get involved with me until I knew what I was dealing with," Kaleigh revealed.

Grant could understand that logic. She had her sisters, but she didn't know if he would stay or run. "Do you remember the first time I carried you to the emergency room? I was so afraid for you, but I was also so thankful that I was there. God put me in that restaurant at that moment for you. I held you and knew then that I never wanted to let you go. That's why I pushed so hard for you to be my real estate agent." Grant paused, took a deep, cleansing breath, then continued when he saw the confusion on Kaleigh's face.

"I have a confession. I selected this house to purchase because it is where we had our first date. I also remember the light in your eyes when you talked about the features of the house. You would get so excited when you walked into a room and saw crown molding." Grant paused, looking at her for any reaction. Her face was inviting and loving and simply beautiful. "I want you to live there with me in that house."

"Grant, I don't know what to say. You bought a mansion with me in mind?" Then, as if the fog finally cleared from her head, she realized what he really said. "You want us to live there together? As in, get married?"

"Yes! Kaleigh Patience Hammond," Grant gave her hand a little squeeze, then bent down on one knee. "I want you to be my wife. Will you marry me?"

"Yes! Yes! Yes! Over and over…Yes!"

Suddenly the door burst wide open and in rushed Janice, Regina, Todd, and Karmyn. Grant laughed at the group. They were all screaming and immediately grabbed her away from Grant to hug and kiss her. Todd was jumping up and down, imitating the women causing everyone to laugh.

A few hours later, the real estate papers were signed, and the McCarter mansion was now owned by Dr. Grant Hawkins and officially renamed the Hawkins Estate. Kaleigh wanted to tell her other sisters about her engagement and show them the house. Grant had given her the extra key and instructed her to begin decorating how she saw fit. Kaleigh called to invite her sisters to her soon to be home. Grant had some things to take care of before meeting with her at the house.

When she arrived, Grant was waiting for her on the front steps.

"How did you get here before me?" Kaleigh smiled.

"Trade secret," he responded.

He whispered in her ear as she crossed the threshold, "The next time we enter this house together, I will be carrying you through as my wife."

She giggled like a schoolgirl and turned to kiss the man who brought her so much happiness.

In the kitchen, they were greeted by her family and Grant's family, who were already holding glasses of champagne.

"To another engagement! Congratulations!" the group cheered.

Chapter 14

The ballroom was exquisitely decorated for the wedding reception of Mr. and Mrs. Simon Sharpe. Kaleigh was double-checking the place settings and making sure the wedding coordinator had the last-minute details. Everything had to be perfect for her older sister. She was going to check the reception music playlist with the DJ when she felt a warm breath on the back of her neck.

"You look beautiful," Grant cooed in her ear before placing the softest kiss to her neck.

"I'm not even dressed yet," Kaleigh pulled the belt tighter around her waist. She had finished with hair and make-up but was still wearing the bridal party robe that had *Maid-of-Honor* emblazoned on the back in crystal rhinestones.

"Even in this robe, which by the way, is *waaay* too short for you to be out in public wearing, you are simply breathtaking," he teased.

Grant always looked at her with passion and love. Kaleigh blushed whenever he gave her compliments, which was all the time.

"Thank you," she moved that non-existent piece of hair behind her ear. "What are you doing here? I thought we were going to meet at the church."

"I am wherever my woman is," he pulled her close. "Are you riding to the church with the bride?"

"I think I should. I am the maid of honor."

"Yeah, I guess you should." He kissed her cheek. "But, after the ceremony, you're all mine, all night."

"I'm hoping I make it through the entire reception," Kaleigh said to him with a look of concern.

"How are you feeling? Any pain?"

"Nothing I can't handle for my sister."

"Good. Can I at least walk you back to your suite?"

"Sure, if you help me find Nick. He is Simon's best man, and I need to make sure he has the rings and the marriage certificate."

Grant released her from his embrace and allowed her to lead the way. "I just saw him heading toward the bar."

"The bar! Oh no! He can't start drinking yet," Kaleigh grasped Grant's hand and walked faster in the direction of the hotel bar.

"I hate to tell you this, but I think all of the men have been drinking," Grant laughed at the face of disapproval she made.

They walked toward the bar near the back of the hotel lobby and stopped short when she saw Karmyn and Nick in a solid lip lock. Instead of busting her sister right there, they tip-toed backward and around the corner.

"I thought they hated each other?" Grant asked.

"They do. At least they have been doing a great job faking it. I'm not sure what I just saw, but you have to promise not to say a word to anyone. Not Kyna, not your siblings, especially John."

"My lips are sealed, promise." Grant mimicked zipping his lips, locking and throwing away the key.

Somehow she was not comforted by that action. Kaleigh made Grant go to the groom's hotel suite and check for the rings and marriage certificate. She couldn't trust that the men would be responsible since they had been drinking. Grant returned with the items, and Kaleigh entrusted the rings to the wedding coordinator until before the ceremony.

At exactly 4:00 p.m., the bridal party arrived at the church, fifteen minutes after the groom and his groomsmen. Simon appeared to be sober, but that wasn't saying much for the others. The wedding coordinator was strict and had the entire ceremony planned down to the minute. She was very efficient and serious about her job.

The men were greeting guests at the front door while the women were in the choir room, completing their last-minute make-up and hair touch-ups.

"In 30 minutes, my oldest baby will be married," Kyra cried as she fixed Karleigh's veil.

"Mom, please don't cry. She did the same thing to me," Karmyn laughed.

"At least Karleigh is having a wedding; you only had a reception for me to cry at. And I will cry again when Poe gets married, and at Kyna's wedding, and when you get married, again."

"Mom, please. Been there, done that," Karmyn rolled her eyes at her mother and walked to a mirror on the other side of the room.

Kaleigh whispered for only Karmyn to hear, "Maybe sooner than you think." She laughed at the expression that Karmyn made.

"I think I'm going to be sick," Karleigh clenched her stomach.

"Quick, somebody get her some crackers and water," Kyra waved to one of the bridesmaids. "You just sit down over here, baby."

Kaleigh started laughing. "I hope I'm not this bad when I get married."

The door swung open. "10 minutes ladies, let's get ready." The coordinator was in and out like a flash of light.

"Poe, when your time comes, I promise to laugh just as hard at you," Karleigh told her. "Come on ladies, let's pray."

All the women in the room gathered together and held hands. Kyra began the prayer by giving thanks to God for her daughters.

The ceremony was beautiful, and Kaleigh only felt like passing out once. She had stashed some crackers and a few bottles of water behind the floral arrangements on the altar. Once the ceremony ended, and the guests emptied the church, the bridal party had to stay behind for pictures. Staying true to his word, Grant remained in the sanctuary the entire time, never taking his eyes from Kaleigh.

*****

She was absolutely breathtaking; he released a slow breath. "She's so beautiful," Grant said low, under his breath. He didn't realize that Nick was sitting in the pew behind him.

"Yes, she is. Karleigh is not bad looking, either," Nick joked.

Grant turned to Nick and laughed, "I doubt we are talking about the same woman."

"Probably not." Nick patted Grant on the shoulder and returned to take more pictures.

Kaleigh smiled at him from her posed looks. Grant knew her different expressions, and he could tell she was handling her pain very well. Even with the best diet and medications, she still had flare-ups. Her determination to manage her Lupus like a fighter was just another reason on a long list of things he admired about Kaleigh.

"And what is that look for?" Kaleigh asked from her spot, still taking pictures.

Grant hadn't realized how transparent he was when it came to Kaleigh. "I was just thinking that this will be us in a few months."

They finished with group photos, and Kaleigh joined Grant in the pew.

"It was a beautiful ceremony," she said, watching the couple take more pictures.

"You are beautiful," Grant gushed.

She tucked her head again. She would never get used to his open admiration of her. "Well, we should head to the reception."

"Did you grab your snacks from behind the flowers?" Grant asked.

"You saw that? They were really for Karleigh, but I needed it more," Kaleigh admitted.

"I was only watching you, so I don't think anyone else noticed."

Grant stood to help Kaleigh with her bouquet, snacks, and shoes when they heard raised voices coming from the back of the church.

"Stay away from me! I hate you," Karmyn yelled.

"You're neurotic. Bipolar or something. Get some counseling," Nick stormed off.

The sisters looked from one to the other and laughed hard and long.

Lisa Washington

SPECIAL DEDICATION

A few years ago, I met a woman at church who, after many conversations, told me she suffered from Lupus.   I had heard of the disease but didn't know much about it. A few years later, I met two more women who also suffer from Lupus, and I started to learn more.

Lupus is a chronic (long-term) disease that can cause inflammation and pain in any part of your body. It's an autoimmune disease, which means that your immune system — the body system that usually fights infections — attacks healthy tissue instead. (www.lupus.org) There is no cure for Lupus.

My friend Ashley Nicole was open and honest with me about her struggles to finding a diagnosis and her life today, living with this mystery disease. She has taught me so much about the disease and how it affects people differently.

This book is also dedicated to Ashley Gatlin, Barbara Lowery, and Paula Glover.   Women whose strength outshine their daily struggle.

For more information about Lupus, Visit www.lupus.org.

A portion of book sales will be donated to the Lupus Foundation of America.

ABOUT THE AUTHOR

Lisa Washington is a Contemporary Christian Fiction author and a serial entrepreneur. She is the co-founder of the Washington Way LLC, which is the umbrella company for Washington Way Publishing, Washington Way Travel, Washington Way Financial and Ms. Lisa Weddings.

Her first novel *When You Least Expect It* received an African American Literary Show Award for Best Christian Fiction. *More Than You Know and Love Lifted Me*, were both nominated and Top Ten Finalist for an Author Elite Award.

Lisa Washington was born and raised in Detroit, Michigan. After serving in the United States Navy, she went on to obtain a Bachelor of Arts degree from Wayne State University, an MBA degree from Averett University and an MFA degree in creative writing from Butler University. She now resides in Georgia with her husband.

Lisa Washington

ALSO BY LISA WASHINGTON

THE FAITH SERIES

When You Least Expect It

More Than You Know

Love Lifted Me

MY SISTERS KEEPER SERIES

Karleigh – A Story of Faith

Kaleigh – A Story of Patience

Kyna – A Story of Love (Coming 2021)

Karmyn – A Story of Hope (Coming 2021)

I hope you enjoyed reading about Poe and Grant. I can't wait for you to read more about Kyna and Karmyn. Stay connected with us for new releases, exclusive offers, free online reads and so much more.

Subscribe to my newsletter
www.authorlisawashington.com

Don't forget to follow and like us on
Facebook - @authorlisawashington
IG - @authorlisawashington
Pinterest - authorlisawashington